ANGELA QUARLES

Unsealed
ROOM PRESS

This is a work of fiction. Names, characters, places, and incidents either are the product of the author's imagination or are used fictitiously. Any resemblance to actual events, locales, or persons, living or dead, is purely coincidental, except where it is a matter of historical record.

DESERVING IT
Copyright © 2018 Angela Trigg
Developmental editing by Gwen Hayes
Line editing by Erynn Newman
Copy editing by Julie Glover
Cover photography: Wander Aguiar
Cover design: Sara Eirew

Unsealed Room Press
Mobile, Alabama

First Print Edition

978-0-9969460-5-6

Advance praise for *Earning It* by Angela Quarles

"Sizzles with heat, sparkles with charm...you'll savor every sexy, emotion-packed moment!"
— Julie Anne Long, USA Today best selling author of the Hellcat Canyon series

"Fun and flirty, EARNING IT is a winner!"
— Avery Flynn, *USA Today* best selling author of *The Negotiator*

"Get ready to swoon hard for a Navy SEAL! Angela Quarles' first contemporary romance is hot and funny and delivers everything I want in a sexy read. This series is a feast of military and sports heroes—the best possible combination for romance readers!"
— Ainsley Booth, *USA Today* bestselling author of *Prime Minister*

"Sweet and steamy, Earning It is a super fun take on the mistaken identity theme set against an unusual sports romance backdrop. A great read!"
— Kate Meader, *USA Today* bestselling author of the Hot in Chicago series

"Pepper and Luke sizzle...my e-reader almost caught fire during a few sexy scenes. This read was sweetness and smolder with just the right dash of swoon. Whip-smart writing and sly humor abounds-simply my favorite kind of read! Angela Quarles is an up-and-coming contemporary romance writer to watch." — Lia Riley, author of the Off the Map and Hellions Angels series

"...a beautiful feel good romance..."
— Keeana with Bookalicious Babes Blog

ALSO BY ANGELA QUARLES

As You Wish
Steam Me Up, Rawley

Must Love series
Must Love Breeches
Must Love Chainmail
Must Love Kilts
Must Love More Kilts

Stolen Moments series
Earning It
Risking It

To those who love sexy accents

1

Conor

"Fuck my arse, but this is deadly, yeah."

This lovely sentiment greets me as I round the corner into the Atlanta hotel's continental breakfast area. The speaker? Patrick, the only other Irishman on the hurling team besides myself.

"Family hotel," I mutter.

The smell of fresh-brewed coffee, browning waffle batter, and maple syrup is so thick, I might as well be swimming through the lot of it.

"Well, ya haven't had a taste of these, have ya?" Patrick lifts a half-eaten cinnamon roll.

I survey the room. Except for one family on the far side, the men's and women's teams have claimed all the tables. Everyone's knackered but wired from our epic win in yesterday's playoffs. Some even won their girl—Aiden strolls in with a woman who, if the fast-flying rumors are true, he's head over arse about. Jane, I think.

And the too-pale bowser moving like an old man on his last painkiller? That's Paolo. One of the lads pulls out a chair for the sorry bugger with an exaggerated by-your-leave wave. The loud scrape of the chair legs makes more than one of them wince. "Shoulda stuck to beer, man. Jager isn't for pussies."

"Fuck you," Paolo growls, but he gingerly sits and cradles his forehead as if his head's made of glass.

Jaysus. Being captain of this team can be a trial sometimes, yeah. "Come here to me, lads. The van'll be arriving in thirty to cart you to the airport. Be out front, mind. I'll not be here rounding you up like a bunch of dossers now."

Aiden, who was nuzzling Jane's neck as he pulled a chair out for her, looks up. "You're not flying out with the team?" He grabs a plate and begins loading up.

I shake my head and grab a plate myself. "Taking a later flight to avoid being with you lot." There's roughly four hours I have before I'm needing to be finding my way to the Atlanta airport, and I'm making the most of it. I wasn't caring for the hint of worry in my sister's voice during yesterday's phone call, which is giving me extra incentive for my presentation tomorrow.

"Ah, Conor, ya redheaded bastard. We're after taking showers, yeah," Patrick yells.

I roll my eyes and load my plate with protein and carbs. "Be out there in thirty."

"You got it, captain." Aiden plunks down with a massive helping of scrambled eggs. The lad smothered his entire plate with the mushy mess. Two slices of American bacon lie on the top.

Plate full and tea in hand, I walk past them. "Enjoy your lax day, lads. We'll be hitting the pitch at the end of the week, mind."

We have the championships to be training for. Amazing this ragged bunch of mostly Americans and Irish-Americans formed a decent hurling team. Their willingness to work hard has paid off something brilliant. The Sarasota Wolfe Tones will be representing the Southeast Division at the championships in Chicago in a bit over a month. Considering how I couldn't leave Ireland fast enough, my fondness for the sport might come as a surprise. But it's the only memory of growing up in the arse-end of Ireland that's keeping me warm.

With a final scold, I turn back for the lift, breakfast in hand. Now, to be working on the Bakerfield presentation. It's the reason I booked a later flight—my peak performance window is late morning and early afternoon, and I don't want to be wasting it with a bunch of raucous, hungover mates when I could be fine-tuning the presentation. And nailing that? Fifteen quid yearly bonus and a surefire path to a promotion. Which ensures my sister never has to be worrying about her farm. Never has to be worrying she doesn't have someone there for her.

Working hard, playing hard, wouldn't that about sum me up? Nothing much else to me.

If I'm avoiding a certain female teammate in the process, that's all gravy, yeah.

CLAIRE

"I'M SORRY, WHAT was our bargain again?" I pick at the seam of the car seat in front of me as the Lyft driver creeps forward another few feet in the bumper-to-bumper traffic on the I-75/I-85 Connector to the Atlanta airport.

The two-hour recommended arrival time passed ten minutes ago. I'm on the phone with my bestie Jane, who was holed up with The Turd after the playoff game, so I didn't get a chance to catch up.

I know perfectly well what our bargain is.

Yeah, I'm stalling.

A frustrated huff comes over the phone. "I did what you asked. I burned a dildo as an effigy, for Pete's sake." Jane's in her car several hours south, heading back to our hometown, Sarasota, Florida.

A male voice laughs, so The Turd must have gone with her instead of flying back with the team.

I snicker. Yeah, the dildo burning had been funny to picture. Jane's the stereotypical librarian you wouldn't think actually exists, but does. I couldn't resist putting that on her list of things she had to do to "break out of her shell" on her trip up here in order to get over The Turd—I mean, Aiden.

I sigh. I really gotta stop thinking of him by that nickname. I saw enough of their interaction yesterday to admit that, yeah, I might've misjudged him.

But while it was fun to put that on her list, I didn't think she'd actually *do* it. I mean, Jesus—it's why I put it on there. And all the other stipulations. Because she wants me to visit my mom, and I said I would *if* she did something for me in return.

And since I reallllly don't want to visit my mom, I made the list impossible for a recluse like Jane to fulfill.

Yeah, that backfired. Plus she ended up getting together with Aiden instead of getting over him.

"I'm holding you to it, Claire."

I trace a star pattern on the window as the Midtown Atlanta skyline inches past. "Yeah, yeah, okay." My voice is all whatever, but hah, not my insides. They're all fuck-shit-no with a big fat dollop of guilt and shame.

"Where are you? I thought your flight left an hour ago?" she continues.

"I didn't fly out with the team. Booked a later flight." I didn't go down to breakfast for the same reason I booked this later flight—Conor. Instead, I got up early and met a college friend for brunch in Gwinnett County. Which…now looks as if it was a stupid move as another minute passes and we haven't mooooved.

Stupid Atlanta traffic. I pull up my Delta app and check in.

"Oh. Okay. See you later this week?"

"It's a date." Thankfully Jane doesn't probe about my later flight—which is so Jane—but lately she seems to be more perceptive about my secret.

That secret?

Oh, just that I have the unhealthiest crush on the men's team captain, one hunky Irish ginger named Conor. With me as the captain of the women's team. Yeah, yeah, cliché. I get that. It's just painful. And downright pitiful. Sometimes I'm sick of myself, because I've had it bad for him ever since the women's team was formed. He walks onto our practice field in those short Irish shorts, thigh muscles bunching and flexing during the drills, and I swear to God my back straightens, my heart beats in a giddy rhythm, and I'm super aware of where he is at all times. And so I'm acutely conscious of where his attention is *not* directed.

I'm the tough jock captain of the women's team in all her unfeminine glory, with grass stains on my knees instead of the latest fashionable stain on pouty lips. Which doesn't do it for him. Which is fine. Sort of. But I refuse to change to appeal to him, so if it's just lusting after him from afar, then so be it.

Ages later, the Lyft driver drops me at Departures. With no bag to check, I head straight to security, and after getting the pat-down, I hustle to the people mover. Alternating between watching the minutes tick by on my phone and the sign indicators on the mover, the doors finally swish open onto C Terminal, and I jog through the crowd to the Up escalators. All but one is packed, so I dash to the one where people are standing along the side. My flight's boarding, and despite being in great shape, my calves are burning as I power up the moving steps. Also, the exhibition games yesterday did a number on my ankles, and there might possibly be a blister forming on the ball of my foot. *Dammit.*

I ignore my body's complaints, and when I get to the top of the escalator, of course the airport is following the rules by having anyone in a hurry assigned to the last gate. I swerve and dodge, my rolling suitcase bobbing and weaving with me on its little wheels. I'm the only one running, and navigating through the crowd—anticipating their trajectories and adjusting my path—is kinda like how it is on a long run down the field when you've got the *sliotar* and are aiming for the goal.

Finally, I reach the end. My gate doesn't have a long line. In fact, no one is in line to board. *Shit.*

I collapse my upper body against the check-in gate's countertop. "Have you closed off boarding?" I get out between gasps.

"No, ma'am."

Ma'am? I'm only friggin' twenty-six.

The overly made-up woman smiles. "Your flight's been delayed forty-five minutes. Weather in Savannah is holding up the plane. The hurricane's weather system is affecting a lot of flights on the Eastern Seaboard."

"Oh good. Okay."

Now I can catch up with myself. I'd forgotten about the hurricane, though. Which, ha-ha, is named Claire.

I limp off. Damn. I really need to tape my ankles. I stroll down the concourse, searching for a nook, corner, unused room, anything to give me the space and relative privacy to shuck off my socks and shoes.

While I don't care what people think of *me,* I don't want to be rude, and I guarantee you no one wants to see the blisters or what could possibly be a blackened toenail, courtesy of a particularly nasty play yesterday.

Up ahead is a snack vendor, and a banana nut muffin catches my eye. I get in line.

While there, I see the perfect spot for the foot inspection. Some might just use a bathroom, but I make it a point to only use a bathroom for, well, going to the bathroom. Nothing else. Not anymore anyway. It's also why I'm getting the muffin—as a former bulimic, I've learned to listen to my body. When it wants something, I get it. With no judgment.

I hand over my money, nab my muffin, and scoot around the partial wall. The closest people are enough of a distance away, and in front of me is a floor-to-ceiling glass wall with a lovely view of asphalt and planes and clear blue skies.

I plop down on the carpeted floor, set my muffin to the

side, zip open my carry-on, and fish around for my tape. The first couple of away games, I didn't bring anything other than the standard travel supplies—clothes, shoes, toiletries. Now I pack a small sports first-aid kit, with tape, Bengay, and other items I, or my teammates, might need.

I yank my shoes and socks off. The nail on my big toe glares back at me, black and purple.

I find the end of the tape and pull, winding it round and round both ankles to support them better. Okay, next—blister investigation. I pull my left foot up to my face. Yep, a blister's forming but hasn't popped. No need for Neosporin. Which, of course, I have too. Just a Band-Aid then.

A startled noise has me looking up, my foot still right up in my face as if I'm smelling it. The one with the black toe. And my heart does a weird squeeze-drop.

Yeah, I said I didn't care what people thought of me or what I was doing. And I don't.

Except for *him*.

Because standing right there with his duffel and a computer bag slung over his shoulder is Conor.

A full body flush of embarrassment and desire washes over my skin.

Which I quickly tamp, because WTF? So what if I look like an unfeminine lump with ugly feet. One of which—dammit—I'm still holding right up in my face.

I let my foot drop with a clunk.

Conor, Conor, Conor. He was supposed to be on the earlier flight with the rest of the team.

He looks baffled for a second, rooted to the ground, staring at me and my legs sprawled out on the carpeted floor. I suppress a sigh because he's the unattainable one. Over six feet of muscle, broad shoulders, and dark red hair against his pale skin, complete with a sprinkling of friggin' freckles. His hair is sticking up in curly waves, and just like the first time I ever saw him, I want to run my fingers through them. His delicious red hair can't be contained on the top of his head, though—Conor has a nice trim beard. Not one of those hipster beards—just full enough to be manly but soft, and not all mountain-man-I-can-hide-a-squirrel-in-here.

Straight nose, strong jaw. Aaaaand that nose and part of his lip just wrinkled. Yep, just caught sight of my feet. Lovely.

"What's news?" he asks. Oh, and I mentioned he's Irish, right? Cuz, yeah, his accent doesn't do it for me *at all*.

Ugh. It totally does. Lilts right up to my lady parts and gives 'em a little tingle.

"Taping my ankles, what does it look like?" Okay. That came out more harshly than I'd have liked, but c'mon.

He puts his hands up in a whoa-Nelly move, his gaze darting to my legs and away. And back. And away—like a car wreck he knows he shouldn't gawk at but can't help it. He backs up. Leaving me alone with my ugly feet.

2

"DELTA FLIGHT 4815 to Sarasota has been canceled," a feminine voice squawks over the speaker.

Bloody hell. I slap the lid down on my laptop and shove it into my messenger bag. Finally I'd found a spot away from screaming kids and other passengers hollering into their mobiles.

My first attempt at finding a quiet corner was a feckin' disaster—the last thing I needed was the image of Claire all...bendy to be plaguing my thoughts while I worked on the presentation. Which is done. It is. I've been obsessing on it most of the day at a nearby Starbucks. I should be letting it go, but I can't. So much is riding on nailing it that I can't stop crawling through every line and slide to ensure I made the most of what I've got. When I arrived at the airport, I was that glad of a delay. But canceled?

I hoof it over to the gate desk, which is absolutely mobbed. When it's my turn, the agent patiently explains Hurricane Claire touching down on the South Carolina coast, and there's not another plane to Sarasota that'll be ready tonight.

Shite. "What's the earliest flight you can be getting me on?"

After some rapid clicking, she hands me back a new

boarding pass. "First flight at 8:44 a.m."

I readjust my rucksack and push away from the counter. Since the flight's only a little over an hour, I'll still make my presentation. Walking past the others in line, it's Claire I spot. "What a mess, yeah?"

She nods and returns to her mobile.

What else should I be expecting? She's always self-contained and low on the drama, even with the fuckton of barbs she has guarding her. When I first met her, she crowded my head with fantasies of her, but at our league's first away game in Chicago, she made it clear she wasn't looking at me that way and I shut that shite down. I don't go in much for relationships and definitely not for pushing if she's giving me back-off signals. And the look on her face earlier? A clear *go away with your hairy eyebrows*. Being smart, I did.

I whip out my mobile because it's a place to crash I'm needing. I do *not* want to be resting my head at the airport.

Q

CLAIRE

I GIVE AN I'm-cool nod to Conor as he walks by. His hair's even spikier than usual, as if he's been yanking on it, proving he's as frustrated as the rest of those around me.

I quickly push accept on my phone app for a room close by—as soon as the cancellation was announced, I started searching. The choices were few, especially at a price I could afford near the airport.

"Your boarding pass, please?"

I glance up at the gate agent who, despite the chaos, has every hair in place and maintains her professional poise. After a few moments, she hands me a new one. "You're on the 8:44 a.m. flight."

"Thank you. No vouchers for a hotel stay?"

"I'm sorry. We're not giving them out tonight."

Well, dang. I tuck everything into my purse and roll my carry-on down the concourse. Apparently ours wasn't the only flight canceled, because the hall is already filling up with people propping up against the wall, or even lying down.

Up ahead, Conor's familiar frame and gorgeous hair are hunched over his phone, a scowl marring his forehead.

I stop beside him, my fingers gripping the carry-on handle. "Did you find a room?"

He glances up. "Everything's booked solid as St. Peter's Rock. Looks like we're camping here."

He must see my guilty expression, because he straightens. "You bagged the last room, didn't ya?"

I swear to God, his Irish accent acts like some kind of aphrodisiac, rolling over me in seductive waves. His *th*'s come out as *t*'s, so *everything* is *everyting* with a little aspiration that's like little happy sighs to my ears. Gah.

"Yep. Looks like I got it just in time. Surely there's some closer in to the city?"

He frowns. "And why would I be wanting to venture out so far? What passes for motorways here would have the devil saying his Hail Marys, and I can't be risking my morning flight."

"8:44?"

"Yeah." He surveys the concourse, the muscles in his jaw bunching. Which—*gah*—does some really hot things to the intensity of his manly face.

I swallow, trying to work some moisture into my throat. "You might be able to rent a car. It's about an eight-hour drive, so you'd get there about the same time."

He shakes his head. "You Americans always thinking it's no bother driving to hell and back in a day. Tempting, as I'm not looking forward to my rucksack for a pillow, but it's work tomorrow and I need some sleep."

"Can't you call in? They'd understand, I'm sure."

His face is always set in serious lines, but it now it grows harder, fiercer. "Yeah, that'd be grand, what with me being the one who's supposed to be giving a big presentation."

Yeah, that would make it tough. I'm fighting the pull to let him stay in my room despite it being only a double. His frustration—I can *feel* it push against me, begging me to make it better for him, but I straighten my spine.

I learned the hard way to ignore my sensitive side, the one that wants to make everyone else comfortable and happy, even if it goes against my own wishes. But I also try not to be an asshole, so it's a fine line to straddle.

He scrubs his hand through his hair and locks his gaze on me.

Shit. Don't ask. Don't ask.

"Listen. This presentation I'm making. It's kind of a big deal. Can I crash with you? I'll be a perfect gent, I swear by all that's holy. I need a good night's sleep is all."

My heartbeat goes all sluggish, and I dart my gaze around as if in search of escape. *Shit.*

Being empathetic sucks. It makes it hard at times like this. But God. No way. Sharing a room with him is the last thing I want—pure torture. Can you imagine? Me. Trying to deal with all that masculine hotness in the same room?

You might wonder what's so bad about that. Well, let me tell you. I have these walls for a reason—that empathic, deep feeling shit? Makes it tough to be in a relationship without getting steamrolled. So you either get me with my armor, or not at all.

And clearly he doesn't like armor-me. We've played in the same league sport for three years now, and he's never given the slightest hint that he's interested. Knowing me, I won't be able to hide my feelings, and one of two things will happen, both of them problematic.

Either he'll be like some guys and not turn down an opportunity for sex. Or he'll reject the idea. I can't do casual sex. Not with him. I just know I won't be able to maintain my armor. I'll start to *feel*. And I'll start changing for him.

And if he rejects the idea, I might feel the pull to change too.

No. Just no.

Don't get me wrong—I can have casual sex. I don't sleep around a ton or anything, but I have no trouble asking for what I want. When the stakes are low and my armor can stay in place.

It's easy when you don't let yourself care.

He steps forward, adjusting his bag's shoulder strap, his green-eyed gaze locked onto mine like some Irish tractor beam, trying to pull me in to his will. "Really. A soft bed's all I'm after. I'm not looking to get in your knickers. It's conked I am."

See? He's not interested.

"I, um, can't. I have…I have some nightly routines. Aaaand morning ones. Trust me, you don't want to be in a room with me."

God, that was lame. His forehead wrinkles, and his eyes take on a confused, unfocused look. He glances up and down my body. Probably trying to picture what the hell my stupid routines could be. *Heck if I know either, bud.*

I could cap it off with a reminder of my ugly feet, but there's only so much I can do in the name of scaring him off.

He leans back against the wall, his movements relaxed, though I still detect tension in his broad shoulders. His duffel drops to the floor. "Yeah, don't be troubling yourself. Probably for the best and all."

Probably for the best? What does *that* mean?

CLAIRE

THIRTY MINUTES LATER, I tap my keycard against the box above the door handle. The green light blinks on my third try. God, I'm exhausted. The guilt riding shotgun with me on the short Lyft drive here doesn't help either. Conor's probably tossing and turning on the cold floor of Concourse C right now because my pansy ass couldn't handle sharing a room with him. Ugh.

I shove my bag inside and ease into the room, plopping my purse onto…a kitchen counter?

I look around the room. *High five*. I scored an executive suite, complete with a galley kitchen and dining room table that doubles as a computer desk, with USB and Ethernet plugs handy.

To the left, I step into a huge-ass bathroom. Seriously. The bathroom alone would be a studio apartment in New York. Beyond the kitchen is just a couch and flat screen TV. Huh? I wander farther in, and that's when I see another room to my left, which has a king bed and another flat screen TV. Somehow I got upgraded.

In the living room, I switch on the TV and head to the couch. A suspicion forms, and I almost don't confirm it, because then I know what I'll feel compelled to do.

But apparently, I don't know…curiosity? A suppressed desire to torture myself by having him over? Whatever it is, I step over to the sofa and lift the cushions.

Shit.

Yep. Sofa bed.

Conor's face as I walked away flashes across my mind, part lost, part resigned, and a whole lot tired.

Jesus. He just wants a place to rest comfortably so he'll be fresh for some big meeting. I'm being ridiculous. And selfish. I'm *not* weak-willed. Not anymore.

CONOR

FUCK ME. I punch my rucksack for the third time and switch

to my other side, hip bone jarring against a floor that's gone harder than a stone's heart. I could be sharing a room right now with Claire. Rooms usually have some kind of chair, and that's gotta be better than this poxy floor.

Because I'd definitely take the chair. Not the bed with her in it. Not with her next to me. Laid out. Both of us comfortable. And it'd be one of those small doubles, and we'd accidentally bump into each other and murmur awkward apologies.

Heat curls through me, and my mind's conjuring Claire stretched out on her side, her arm resting over her hip, with one finger crooking and urging me closer. To her.

I give a start and shut that shite down fast.

She's not interested, eejit. Claire is direct and not afraid of saying what she wants.

At first, when I heard she had a room, all I could think about was the presentation and how badly I needed to do well so I can be helping my sister with the family farm. But then as her excuses piled up, it was a slap in the face, yeah—a reminder of every one of our prickly encounters. Gets me frustrated, it does, and then I'm saying stupid shite like, *Probably for the best*. Probably for the best doesn't get a place for my head to be resting, now does it?

My mobile beeps a text alert. I fish it out from the back pocket of my jeans. It's from Claire: *Room 151*

Triumph's surging through myself, especially when the mobile dings again, this time with the address of her hotel.

Effin' fantastic.

I jump up and grab my rucksack. Now I'll be having some decent sleep at last. We'll both be so knackered, there'll be no energy for our uneasy dancing.

It doesn't take but twenty minutes, and I'm knocking on Room 151. A minute passes, then the door opens and Claire appears. She's draped in an oversized T-shirt and baggy men's boxers.

Well, that's absolutely fantastic—such form-disguising clothes shouldn't be a turn-on, but fuck if the lad in my trousers doesn't twitch. *Down, boyo*.

I'm knackered. That's all it is. And seeing her in sleepwear is melding with my earlier fantasy of us sharing the same bed.

"Hey. Well, thanks for letting me crash here." I look past her, my gaze searching out my goal—my spot to sleep.

"No problem. Come in." She pads into the main part of the room and points. "Here's the kitchen."

Who feckin' cares? But I dutifully nod.

A weird tautness permeates the air. With her standing there, vulnerable in her baggy clothes, I feel every bit of my six-foot-two, two-hundred-pound size. As if it's pushing into her personal space. And that personal space is this whole room.

Jaysus, I'm being a tool. If I hadn't acted whiney as a two-year-old in wet nappies, she wouldn't be bailing me out of a tight spot.

She's uncomfortable, that much is clear, pointing out each spot in the room when I just want to know—where am I going to be laying my head?

Her increasing nervousness makes me study her for the first time in a while—she's acting so not like her normal tough persona, and it's making me curious. I've never worried about my size around her, while I *do* feel like some huge mong around other women. Especially shorter ones. But Claire's never seemed to me to be all that intimidated.

It was that strength in her that caught my eye the first time she walked up to me, saying she'd heard about the men's hurling team and was wanting to start a women's equivalent in Sarasota—camogie.

Of course, me being a lad, I also noticed her fantastic tits—the right size for her tall frame, that athletic body of hers, and all those grippable curves. When she proved level-headed, I was caught enough to watch her closely, to see if she was giving the slightest clue that she was interested in me.

Which she didn't.

This behavior, however? This is different.

16

3

JESUS. I'M CHANNELING some flighty chick from a romcom, because here I am pointing to different spots around the suite as if it's my own damn apartment and I'm giving him the grand tour and am nervous about having a hot guy over for a date.

Except he *is* a hot guy, and I *am* nervous.

But it's definitely not a date.

I keep going with the mouth diarrhea and hand flailing as if I have no control over this dorky woman who's invaded my body, because I'm pointing again. "There's the sofa bed. I checked. There are sheets and a pillow in the closet." Aaand I point to the closet. "As well as an extra blanket. If you need it. You know, if you get cold."

The TV gets the finger treatment next. Then I start for the bedroom and pause.

Nope.

No need to have *that* pointed out. I pivot to go past him, but my sudden stop has him right behind me and I'm brushing against his large, hunky body. His strength, his heat, are like a wall up along my side. *Zing.* A bunch of dormant parts of me light up and wave.

I clear my throat, the sound jarring in the quiet of the room.

I wave behind him. "The bathroom's next," I squeak out. Seriously, who *is* this woman?

He cocks an eyebrow but turns and heads there. My body relaxes by degrees as his steps take him from my side.

When the bathroom light hits his gorgeous face, my breath catches. Not at his gorgeous face. That's not a surprise. Nope, it's because the light just reminded me what I left in there. *Shit.*

I sprint forward and hip-check him as if we're opposing players on the field. He grunts, but barely moves. That doesn't stop me, though. I squeeze past his large frame and whip the undies I left hanging to dry over the glass shower wall.

That would be embarrassing enough. But more embarrassing? These are boring white cotton panties.

Maybe I *am* a dork.

I quickly glance sideways at him. He's got too much of the look of feigned concentration on some other part of the wall—yep, he saw.

Oh well.

One night. That's all I have to get through without revealing my feelings for him.

One. Damn. Night.

CONOR

BOLLOCKS. ALL I'M doing tonight is punching feckin' pillows. First, it was my rucksack at the airport as I tried to make it and the floor into a bed for myself. Now, I have a goddamn real pillow and a surprisingly comfortable sofa bed and... I'm wide awake, staring into the darkened ceiling like a bloody muppet.

I mean, what the fuck?

Is it nerves for my presentation? Yeah, a bit of it, but that doesn't usually prevent me from falling asleep, especially after playing hard over a weekend. I'll get that bonus and secure my sister's farm, yeah.

But as I flip to my other side and picture Claire and how awkward it was when I arrived and we were both readying for bed, I think I know why. And I'm regretting coming here. Because a thread of unease is winding through me at the idea of getting with Claire.

The bleeding truth is, I'm not one for long-term relationships. I left Ireland to escape the disaster of my personal life. When your only girlfriend is someone who knew you your whole life, and the entire village was thinking you were getting hitched, it fucking guts you when she finds you lacking, yeah. Up till that moment, I was telling myself that my mam leaving when I was a lad wasn't on me. But it's hard-going to convince yourself of that after being unceremoniously dumped. Hard-going not to question everything that's happened to you leading up to that moment.

Just the idea of opening myself up to Claire has me tied up in feckin' knots.

Jaysus. What a whiney man-child I'm after being. I'm spinning what-ifs in the air like it's my life depending on it. My brain's knackered to be thinking Claire has any interest in me for the long term, much less for some riding in the sheets.

I've set the alarm for five a.m. When that alarm rings—and Mother Mary do I pray it snatches me from a deep sleep and doesn't find me still staring at this dark ceiling—we'll be gone away from each other and getting on with ourselves.

CONOR

M<small>Y MOBILE'S BLARING</small> an obnoxious, repetitive sound, waking me from sleep. I groan and lean over to the end table. The room, shrouded in the dark gray of pre-dawn, slowly swims into focus. Slapping my hand around the table finds me the hard shape of my mobile.

"Enough with it, yokes," I mumble at the sound, desperate to end the noise. Through the bedroom door, Claire's mobile is making the same blaring sound.

At least I'd fallen asleep.

It's an emergency alert. The words are staring up at me. The hurricane made landfall north of Savannah and is heading…to Atlanta?

I have some text alerts too, one from Delta. I pull that one up first.

"Fuck," I groan. The airport is after shutting down all flights in and out. We're stuck in Atlanta for the day at the least.

Through the bedroom door, Claire grunts the same word of frustration. I smile. Just then my five o'clock alarm rings, and I shut it off.

What the effin' hell am I going to do now? I pull up the weather app. The whole Southeastern United States is covered in a big spiral. Well, there goes Idea Number One—it's not a rental car we'll be driving straight through a hurricane.

We. My mind's going straight to *we*.

Christ bleeding on the cross.

The bedroom door snicks open, light from her room bleeding in, and Claire pokes her head out, her brown hair sticking out in tangles. She has a crease along one cheek. She blinks at me and rubs an eye. "Did you see the news?" Her voice is groggy, and she looks adorable in her sleep-rumpled state.

I sit up. "Yeah." I run my hand over my scalp. "I thought hurricanes only hit your coastal cities?"

She leans against the doorframe. She doesn't realize it, but the action pulls her baggy shirt up, exposing a sliver of smooth stomach. My dick chubs up a little.

"Yeah, this is a little unusual. It'll probably lose strength, but it's happened once before that I know of—Hurricane Opal back in the 90s. Hit Atlanta just after being downgraded to a tropical storm, if I remember right."

"Ain't that savage," I say as I make sure my blanket is covering the important—*growing*—bits. I must have been out of my bleeding skull to be thinking last night that she was uncomfortable because she was attracted to me.

"Yeah." She looks back to her mobile and rubs the sleep from her eyes with her other hand. "I'm booking the room for two more nights just in case."

"Grand idea, that. I'll see if some have opened up."

She looks relieved. That shouldn't bother me, but it's doing just that. It's not that I'm thinking I'm some great catch or such a magnetic and fine personality that everyone wants to be near, but the usual lot just find me neutral, not repellent.

"I'll just be ringing work then. My boss'll be needing as much time as possible to rearrange schedules."

I heave out of the bed and fold it up, setting the furniture to rights. I yank the curtains open. While it's still dark out, I can see that it's already bucketing down. The first squalls have hit us. I pull in a deep breath and hit the number on my mobile for my boss.

Conor

TOO WIRED TO go back to sleep after hashing things out with my boss, I hopped in the shower. He wasn't all that pleased with me. While he certainly can't blame me for the weather, he slipped in there an underlying current of blame—if I didn't have this "sport hobby thing," his words, not mine, I wouldn't even be in Atlanta to be getting myself stranded.

For fuck's sake—I think he wants all of his employees to be mindless, no-life drones. He let me reschedule, though, so there's that. I rinse the last of the soap off my body, wrench the taps shut, and yank the towel off the shower door where I'd left it. It's while I'm drying off in vigorous strokes and dressing that my mind spins with how I might be able to salvage this arseways situation. Dressed, I drape the towel around my neck and step out of the bathroom. Only to see Claire, her change of clothes gripped in her hand, her gaze averted.

Feeling every inch of my bulk—inches from her delectable but off-limits body—I slip past her and flip on the telly, running a towel over my damp hair, my mind now latched onto Claire and how we're stuck in Atlanta.

Shite. Because of the call to my boss, I forgot to look for another room. I tap around various sites, searching. Nothing.

I glance around the impersonal room. If we're stuck here much longer, I'll need a laundrette. I've been in Atlanta for a week, and no girl wants a stinky gouger sharing their room. That is, if she'll let me stay. She's already barely tolerating me.

The shower turns on. Bleedin' deadly. She's in there, stepping into the sleek stall, naked. The water sluicing over her curves. Fuck.

I collapse onto the couch and surf through the channels, stopping at the broadcast of the Summer Olympics. It's track and field day, and I settle in to be watching the 100-metre dash.

In front of me, there's a dark red footstool. Or ottoman? It's the same height as the couch seat, but it's covered in pleather. Footstool then. I hike my feet up and stretch back.

The bathroom door clicks open. I can't be helping myself. I glance up. Claire steps out, her hair wrapped in a towel, her robe closed tight around her, her bare legs peeking out below, which, yeah, I've seen on the field, but it's different this time. Like I'm seeing a warrior without her armor.

Fuck. I'm starting to think more about her than my presentation.

She gives me a sheepish curve of the lips, one that acknowledges that we've landed in a hella-awkward situation. Her gaze lands on the telly, and she sharply turns away and heads into the bedroom, closing the door firmly behind her. A distinct chill settles over the room.

In other words, more of the same in the story of our prickly interactions, yeah.

4

CLAIRE

HANDS SHAKING, I close the door.

Crap. Already it's hard dealing with Conor sharing my space, but seeing the Summer Olympics on the TV? Ugh. I grab a brush and pull it methodically through my wet hair.

I have no desire to see the visuals or hear the commentary that is the Summer Olympics. I can't always avoid it, but when I can, I will.

I take my time going through my clothes and selecting what to wear. It's *not* because Conor is here, but because doing so will mean less time seeing the games. It's a reminder of the most painful part of my life. When my mom rode preteen me hard to train for the Olympics. I loved sailing and showed promise, but that's all. I had no desire to make the US sailing team. But did I express my wishes and trample my mom's? No.

Because those forces you hear about on TV—those stage moms who live vicariously through their kid? Yep. That was my mom. The pressure to please and perform messed with my head. And having to wear a swimsuit all the time as I was going into puberty? Hello, fresh hell. Especially when I compared my body with my mom's lithe, model-thin one. I have no idea what my dad looks like, but I'm guessing I took after his side of the family.

I slip on a functional pair of shorts and a T-shirt. The first time I forced myself to throw up was a quick solution to overeating one day when I realized how that would make my body even more unlike my mom's. Had learned the "trick" from a friend. And then…

And then I became overly familiar with the stalls at the Sailing Squadron in Pensacola where I trained, throwing up when no one could hear. The sick thing is, it was working, sort of. Until it didn't.

I made my body so unhealthy that I failed the Olympic trials. My mom and my boyfriend at the time were disappointed. And because I'm empathetic and hadn't yet learned to distinguish someone else's emotions from my own, I felt *every* drop of it.

Somehow, hitting that low point was my salvation. Because I sought help.

But I've never forgiven my mother, or myself, for having to break off with her completely to heal. That's why I won't visit her now, despite my stupid bargain with Jane. Going back would be like revisiting my old, sick, less secure self, and who needs that? I've remade myself, from the ground up. Maybe if I told Jane about my mother, she'd let up on the pressure to visit her. It's just that…it's so hard admitting that weak part of me. Admitting that there was a time in my life when I *wasn't* the strong person I am now.

When I close a drawer after unpacking my whole suitcase and look around for something else to do, I pause. *Whoa.*

I'm hiding in my room.

The unpacking can be kinda-sorta excused because I'll be here for a few days, but, yeah, I'm hiding. This is *not* me.

I roll my eyes and step into the living room. Conor is splayed out on the couch, his large frame taking up a good chunk, his muscled forearms stretched along the back. Thank God he'll be in his own room soon. That is…

"Any luck finding a room?"

He looks up and hits the remote on the TV, shutting it off.

"Looks like you're stuck with me—that is, if you've a mind to keep letting me crash here?"

Crap. Crap. Crap. But I can't kick him out. "Sure. That's fine." I look away. "You hungry?"

"I've a mouth on me, yeah." He stands, and we silently head out the door, down the hall, and to the breakfast buffet area. All the while, his presence is like a warm pressure behind me.

How the hell am I going to get through a full day and another night with him and not expose my feelings?

To distract myself on the way, I text Jane: *Make it okay?*

Almost immediately comes her reply: *Yes. You?*

I tap out a quick update on what's happened, and by then we reach the lobby. Like most mid-priced hotels, the breakfast area is a room off here. It's half full, with most people on the phone as they eat, trying to contact relatives about the storm. The scent of breakfast goodness greets me. Man, I'm hungry. The buffet has a little of everything, and I thread down the line with my plate and pick whatever speaks to me. No judgment. I also snag a glass of OJ and a hot tea.

Back at my table, I spread a napkin in my lap, cut a hunk of melon in half, and bring it to my mouth. I close my eyes as my tongue touches the cool surface and my teeth bite down. The flavor bursts on my tongue like the freshest sunrise. My taste buds sing. I slowly chew it, noting its different flavors, letting them seep into me.

Conor settles across from me, his plate loaded with bacon, eggs, fruit, and a lone sausage patty.

The Olympics are being shown on all the flat screens, of course, but now the bottom third is plastered with updates on Hurricane Claire's strength and trajectory.

"What did your work say?" I ask.

"Was able to get my presentation rescheduled, yeah. Yourself?"

"This week I wasn't scheduled for camp, so that made it easier."

He bites off a piece of bacon and chews, looking at me

with an interest that makes me squirm. "What is it you do?"

"Office manager for the Sarasota Sailing Squadron, but I also teach sailing classes during the summer."

His eyebrows rise. "Huh. Sounds the business. I've never been sailing."

"Seriously?" Excitement percolates through me. Excitement I should *not* be feeling, dammit.

He shakes his head.

"Well, that's a shame, but you can easily fix that when you get back. We have a great bay for sailing." I take another bite, this time of my eggs, savoring them even though they're not the best.

Conor squints at the flat screen in his line of sight. "You know, despite living in Sarasota, I've not experienced a hurricane."

"Lucky." I chuckle. "Ironic it's when you're in Atlanta, more than two hundred miles from the coast."

He turns his face to mine and smiles, completely transforming his face from a good-looking but serious guy to a warm, approachable, hot guy. "And it's named Claire."

Ha-ha. Yeah. To distract myself from all the sexy beamed right at me, I say, "I was six when Hurricane Opal hit Pensacola."

His fork stops halfway to his mouth, and his green eyes latch onto mine.

I laugh and sample some of the other fruit. "I take it you didn't have hurricanes where you grew up?"

"Not as often as your country, though we can be getting some fierce winds off the Irish coast. What's it like?"

I wave a fork. "Every year during hurricane season, we kept a grid map of the Southeastern US, plus a good chunk of the Atlantic, taped to the fridge, and we tracked every storm. Opal was my first hurricane, and I remember it vividly, including where it ended up. We evacuated to some of Mom's relatives in Biloxi, whom I never saw again, so I didn't actually experience it. I remember the prep—mom hiring some guy to board up the house, getting everything movable out of the yard and off the porch, that kind of thing."

"So you've never weathered one as it hit?"

"Nope. Though I've been in my share of tropical storms." I sit back in my chair and take in the flat screen and all of its warnings. "One hit us without warning. The day before it was squalling. I was maybe fourteen? Our sailing instructor didn't cancel lessons that day, saying it'd be good foul weather practice."

"Jaysus." He sets his fork down. "What happened?"

"Well, we all got in our boats to trek across the bay and back. At first it was just a lot of rain. But then, yep, it got bad. Wind scouring us, choppy water, that kind of thing. I was learning to sail a hulled craft, so I and my other two classmates were the safest. The poor kids in their prams had it the worst."

"Their prams?" He laughs. "This is one of those language things, because there's no feckin' way you'll have me believing the poor buggers were in baby carriages out on the water, yeah."

I laugh, though even I can hear the nervous thread in it. This is the longest we've talked in one stretch, and my heart's going *bam-bam-ba*m like it's hopped up on caffeine. "No. Prams are a small type of boat. Super small. Made of wood and seat one. Their tiny masts were snapping like sticks when we were about halfway across, and the instructor had his hands full running around in his speedboat picking up the poor kids. The guys in their lasers helped."

"Lasers?"

"Yep. Another type of boat, sorry. Fiberglass, one-person boat. Super-fast."

"Did you help as well?"

I give a rueful laugh. "Nope. Our mast snapped too. We had an anchor, unlike the others, but the boats were new and the clamps weren't installed yet. So I held onto the anchor line, trying like hell to keep us attached to it, while the wind and waves pushed our boat." I rub my hands down my thighs, the memory still sharp of my palms being rubbed raw by the anchor line.

"Sounds like you handled it well enough."

"Actually, one of the others in the boat was terrified and curled up in the corner crying for his mom, leaving me and the other guy to keep us from tipping." I ended up dating that guy all through high school, that experience bonding us. "It was scary, but the instructor kept zipping by to check on us while he rescued the others. The whole bay was chopping gray waters and shrouded sky."

"Came out of it looking shook, did they?"

My stomach signals it's full, and I push my plate away. "It all ended well, though I don't know how the instructor fared later. Probably got an earful from all the parents. That night it turned into a tropical storm, which became known for a while as the No Name Storm. Lots of folks had boats and belongings ripped away and washing up on shore."

For days afterward, the bay was brimming with jellyfish, making a great incentive for not tipping our boats when we were able to sail again. Since our boat was disabled, I sailed a laser, which is a lot harder to keep from tipping in a strong wind. I was barely able to make the weight for sailing one—a hundred pounds. It was also my first time getting stung by jellyfish, because, yep, I couldn't keep it upright. The memory of leaning out is still vivid, my back arched over the water, my boat almost vertical, and me staring down at the sea of jellyfish and going, *oh shit*.

Conor wipes his mouth with a napkin and leans back. "We didn't live directly on the coast, but Galway gets hit with some fierce weather. There's always reports of a fisherman getting himself lost, trees down, and rivers flooding."

Yeah, sailing and living in Pensacola gave me a healthy respect for Mother Nature. "And speaking of storms, we need to prep for this one. Looks like it will hit us some time tonight."

"What are you suggesting?"

I pull out my cell and search. "There's a Piggly Wiggly nearby. Let's request a Lyft. There's also a laundromat in the same complex. If the power goes out, we'll be glad we washed the clothes we have."

He nods and stands. "Sounds grand."

5

GOOD LORD, IT'S a friggin' madhouse at the Piggly Wiggly in East Point, Georgia. Everyone's panicked, filling up shopping buggies like the Apocalypse is coming, getting those milk sandwiches we Southerners are so famous for. We loaded up the washing machines at the laundromat a couple of doors down, and while they're doing their thing, we ducked in here.

I push the buggy down the bread aisle and grab one of the last loaves. "No sense getting perishables past today in case the power goes out. Can't rely on the hotel having a generator. After that, non-perishable."

Conor keeps pace beside me. "How long are you thinking we'll be stuck here?"

"Who knows? Probably only for a day, but better to be prepared. We can donate what's left to a shelter."

Conor nabs a frozen pizza. Meat and Veggie Lovers. He holds it up by his face with a grin. "For lunch. I say since we're stuck in a hotel room with a hurricane coming at us, we might as well be having some fun with our food choices."

I poke him in the chest as I pass by him. "I like how you think, Mr. McDaid."

He smirks and tosses it into our buggy. In the produce

31

section, I grab some apples. The crunch and juiciness of biting into one calls. In they go.

Food is fuel. Something that took me a while to see.

We tool down the canned food aisle, and Conor grabs some Le Sueur green peas. He reads the label. "Very young small early peas." He snorts. "How many adjectives is it needing to get the point across?"

We banter like this, our choices in sync sometimes with what we pick, but always by method—we're picking things because we *want* them.

Last time I grocery-shopped with a guy was soooo not this. At all. *This* I'm actually enjoying. My boyfriend during my sick time was also training to make the Olympic sailing team, and our trips to the grocery store were fraught with decisions regarding calories and whether it had trans fat or high fructose corn syrup, or whatever chemical was obsessing us at the moment. Not a fun experience. No. Instead, anxiety clogged me up, worrying about whether I was choosing the right thing or how much fat it might add to my thighs.

I don't remember much of that time other than flashes of forcing myself to throw up—secretly and full of shame— but I do remember our shopping trips because it was one of our "couple" things.

Basically, my teenage years were a haze. A haze of me trying to please my mom and my boyfriend, and letting my own wishes and desires be steamrolled by those stronger.

Thank God that's behind me. It took a while to toughen up, to not see others' wishes as superseding mine. Learning to recognize and respect my own emotions.

No one will control me like that again.

We roll down another aisle. Conor squats and holds up a pack of candles, the movement doing some ridiculous things to his thigh muscles. C'mon, it's like he's showing off.

"Definitely." I grab a lighter so I can look away. I spot a pack of cards and throw them in too.

I have to admit, though, working together to prep for this big storm is fun.

Conor

NEVER THOUGHT SHOPPING could be great *craic*, but there it is. Claire's shed some of her awkwardness around me, and I catch myself reacting to her, messing around just for her.

Jaysus. I'm *flirting*. With Claire.

Huh.

But not only am I feeling…playful around her, there's this strange weight missing that's normally hanging on my shoulders. As if being stuck here is giving me the space to relax and have a savage time. As if I'm some kind of prisoner let loose for a whale of a time on an unsuspecting town.

I grab the silver container of Jiffy Pop popcorn and toss it in the trolley, and Claire laughs. Christ, American supermarkets are banjaxed. Popcorn in a tinfoil pouch. The novelty's worn mostly off, though, from the first time I walked into one. There's just so *much* of everything. So many choices for every little thing too. But, yeah, I don't care since I'm bunking off work and having myself some unexpected fun.

Proof of how much I'm farting around?

Claire makes a goofy face while reading a label on a can, and I laugh out loud. Like full on, everyone's-looking-at-me laugh.

Claire stops, and her breath catches. Her eyes slowly lift to mine.

I shift on my feet. "What? Do you think I'm touched?"

"Touched?"

"Crazy."

"I haven't heard you laugh too often. And never like that."

I stare at her. She's right, I know. I'm not one for laughing much. Aiden's the gallery-entertainer on our team, and no one's ever accused me of laughing my cacks off. But I'm also not some emo sap that's as useless as tits on a bull.

Then her words sink in. For her to be saying such a thing means she's been aware of me for longer than I knew, whether I'm laughing or not.

Now I'm the one catching my breath. Especially when she's going scarlet as she must be seeing…what she revealed. And she's that mortified.

All the hairs rise on my skin, and my heart does an odd thump. And then it starts coiling down, stirring my pipe.

Claire's gaze darts to the side. Then she does a strange hop and gets behind the trolley. She wants to play it cool. But I know better now.

Claire's been hiding a secret.

Claire's thinking I'm mighty feen.

Has she been thinking this the whole time, and I was too much of a muppet to notice?

And just like that, the woman I forced from my mind several years ago is back, front and center and fully crowding my thoughts.

Jaysus.

CLAIRE

GROCERIES SPLIT AND paid for, we face an interesting dilemma. We forgot we didn't have a car to put it in. And we still need to pick up our clothes. And while it's not far away to the hotel, it's pounding down rain.

We're staring at the buggy, and then we laugh at the same time. He's got a ton of bags in each hand, and so do I. And we still have bags in the buggy. Thankfully the strip mall has an overhang covering the sidewalk.

Conor heaves his bags back into the buggy.

"What are you doing?"

He gives me a big grin, and my heart does another kick. When he laughed in the grocery store, it made his serious face five years younger. He was beautiful. And I'm seeing that beauty again.

"We don't need to be carrying them yet. We'll just roll this into the laundrette, put our clothes in here too, and then load up the Lyft car when it gets here. I'll give him a bit extra for helping, yeah."

"Sounds like a plan." I place all mine back in and flex my fingers, getting the blood flowing again. "Good thing the only cold item is the pizza."

"And we'll cook that up when we get back." He pushes the buggy down the sidewalk of the strip mall, and we bump it into the laundromat. We get some weird looks, but whatever.

We managed to combine our clothes into one machine for colors and one for whites. Both are done now, so we throw them into the big dryers. It's weird having our clothes mixed together, as if we skipped to some future stage of dating, but I try not to focus too much on that.

We have thirty minutes to wait, so I fish around our grocery bags and pull out the pack of cards. "You ever play Spit?"

His footsteps bring him closer, and he's by my side, and I'm acutely conscious of how close he is to me. "Never heard of it."

I motion to two empty red Formica chairs with a short table between. I love Spit. "Prepare to learn from the master."

He brushes past me, his scent brushing me too, and folds his large body into the tiny chair. "The master, is it now?" He glances up at me.

And I proceed to kick his hot Irish ass at the fast-paced game.

6

Conor

THE LYFT DRIVER pulls up to the curb in front of the launderette and runs out with a massive golf umbrella. Thank
fuck, he helps us load all the scran we bought, as well as
our bag of clothes. Somehow he manages to keep us both
relatively dry.

We scramble into the back seat, and I pull out a twenty,
placing it on his console. "Here's some for helping us, yeah?"

The driver looks down at the bill and grins. "Thanks."

A few minutes later, we pull up under the hotel's awning.
I retrieve a luggage cart from the lobby, and the unloading
goes faster than ever since we don't have to be messing
about with his umbrella. As we wave a farewell to Pete the
driver, I check the time on my mobile. It's almost gone one.
I'd like to give my sister a bell before it gets too late to call
someone in Ireland.

Claire and I make quick work of unpacking all of our
stuff in the kitchen, and I laugh again.

She lifts an eyebrow.

"We have enough to last us two weeks or more, I'm
thinking."

She glances over the mound of bags of taytos, pastries,
and canned goods she's organized along the counter. She

rubs her hands together. "I think you're right."

I chuckle and pull out my mobile, holding it up. "Going to ring my sister, yeah."

She nods and unearths the pizza. "I'll get this started. I'm starving. You?"

"I could eat the lamb of Jesus through the rungs of a chair."

I fall into the couch and punch the icon for my sister.

"Con," Siobhan says when she answers, and I hear the smile in it. Her voice—Christ, every time it's like a tug on my heart—part affection, part bittersweet. I love my sister and would do anything for her, and I miss her. But it comes with some baggage I hate facing every time we're after chatting. Some of that baggage is guilt for leaving her to tend to the family farm after our da passed five years ago.

I couldn't get away from the farm—and Ireland—fast enough. Too many memories. Of my old life, my old culchie self. Thank fuck my sister was ever too young to remember our mother. She only misses her as a concept.

Me? Yeah. I remember the woman. My most vivid memory, and the last I have of her, is permanently seared into my memory bank. The farmhouse seems larger in mind than it would later. The hall going on forever. Dark. And my mam looking down at me, her mouth moving with angry words, most of which I'm not recalling to mind. But one word registered. "Useless." And then the dropping sensation my seven-year-old heart felt. Especially when I woke the next morning to find she'd left us. For good.

CLAIRE

CONOR'S TALKING TO his sister, whom I'm assuming is still back in Ireland judging from some of the things he says.

Beyond him, the picture window highlights a gray world of angry rain, with trees swaying to one side.

The oven dings, telling me it's done preheating, and I slide our pizza in and set the timer.

While our room is larger than a standard hotel room, it's still small enough to hear Conor's conversation. A farm is the main topic, and while his tone's light, he's gone from sitting on the couch to pacing circles around the living room. There's an underlying tension in his voice that I can feel.

Finally he hangs up.

"Everything okay?" I ask.

He pivots quickly but gracefully for such a large guy. "Yeah, just having some…business to be dealing with over the family farm." His accent grew thicker during the phone conversation, and it still has a deeper lilt than usual.

Dammit. It's sexy as hell. "You have a farm in Ireland?"

"My sister holds onto it, yeah."

I pull down two plates. "But it sounds like you're a part of it too?"

He rubs the back of his neck. "It's where we grew up in County Galway, near Kilbannon. A sheep farm. When my father passed, I didn't want to be running it, but my sister did. I signed my share over to her before I left for the States."

"She must love it."

"That she does. Always has. She's trying to strengthen the Galway breed of sheep and took out some loans, which scares the shite out of me."

I search the cabinets for glasses and pull down two. I find silverware in the drawers. "How come?"

"She's my little sister. I'm going to worry, yeah."

I have no idea what that's like, as I'm an only child. And while he's been answering my questions, I get a vibe that he doesn't like to talk about it, so I change topics. "Sounds like your presentation is a big deal."

I hear him moving behind me and glance over my shoulder. He sits at the small dining table and looks down, laying his palms flat down on it. "That it is. Part of my yearly evaluation. If it's bang on, I'll be getting myself a pure savage bonus."

"Savage?"

He leans against the table and crosses his arms, his mouth pulled up at the corner. "Savage as in excellent. Fierce. Big. Still floors me how much tech companies throw around in this country, even in this economy. Bleeding *flahulach* they are. I love America."

I knew he worked at some high-power tech firm, but he didn't strike me as money hungry. "Oh. That's…cool."

He leans back against his chair, his broad shoulders straightening, and looks at me. "Yeah. I want to be paying off my sister's loans she has on the farm, though she doesn't know it yet. And snagging that bonus will leave me standing in line for a promotion."

Okay, *that* fit better into my impression of him. "Now I can see why you wanted to get your beauty sleep last night."

He snorts. "The farm's been in the family for donkey's years." His voice has an odd quality to it, and because I've always been able to easily pick up others' emotions, I can feel a guilt come off him that I'm not even sure he's aware of. And I can see the result—he works as hard as he does to compensate for all that guilt.

But he seems to shake himself, as if he didn't mean to share that much. He pushes away from the table and walks over to the TV, settling into the couch.

Conor

I'm watching some reality show on the telly where these blacksmiths compete to make weapons, and it's hard core. But then it penetrates my thick skull that Claire's cooking the pizza—a whiff of it's after cluing me in—and she's bustling around the table. I lift off the arm of the couch, holding myself up to see. She's setting it?

I hop up. "What can I be doing?"

She pauses, a plate halfway to the table, and glances up. "If you could grab the pizza, I think the timer's about to—"

The timer buzzes, and I hustle over to the kitchen, grab an oven mitt, and slide out the grand gooey goodness. Cheese bubbles expand and pop. The crust is a perfect gold. Feckin' deadly. I place it on the counter and start cutting up the slices.

I glance over my shoulder. Sure enough, she's set two plates—two paper towel napkins are folded and tucked under the rims, with forks and knives on top. She's poured the cola-flavored fizzy drink we purchased into tall glasses. I frown—the formality of the table setting doesn't fit with the tough girl, captain of the camogie team, I've always seen.

"You didn't have to be doing that up. I'd have been perfectly happy to eat sitting on the couch." I don't say that I normally eat standing up in the kitchen.

She glances up. "I like to make meals an event. Doing this helps me savor it, be conscious of it instead of rushing through it unnoticed."

Huh. Okay. "Grab your plate then and be savoring this, yeah." I shove the oven mitt back on and hold up the pizza.

She picks up both plates and brings them over, and we load up. She sets her plate down at her spot. "Is it okay if I turn off the TV?"

I shrug. "Sure. Why not?"

She walks over and turns off the telly and settles herself, placing her napkin on her lap with some care.

Now I'm watching in fascination. I mean, I've seen people eat before this. But she's treating it as if this is some grand do, even though it's just heated-up frozen pizza. She probably was doing the same thing at breakfast, and I wasn't noticing.

She cuts the tip off a slice, purses her lips, and blows on it.

Fuck if my lad doesn't pop my zipper just then.

She takes a bite, the cheese stretching across to the

rest of her slice, and closes her eyes. She looks…she looks *happy*. And then she moans. Now I'm after being seriously chubbed up.

"Mmm, so good," she murmurs.

I look at my slices, which I haven't even touched yet. I bring my plate to the other place setting and pick up a slice, biting into it. It's better than your average frozen pizza, but it's still fucking frozen pizza. So I chew a little more thoroughly and try to taste what she's tasting.

By my third bite, I'm picking out more flavors that I'd normally miss—a hint of some spice, the deep tones of the tomato sauce. Damn, this pizza's *deadly*.

We eat in silence, but it's not awkward. She picks up her second slice and asks, "Is there anything I can do to help you prep for your presentation?"

I stare at her in surprise. "Yeah, thanks, got it done, not that I don't appreciate the offer."

"Do you want to practice it in front of me?"

For some reason, the thought's making me squirm. I've already shared more about my past with her than normal, and this feels like even more, though it's just a dry presentation.

Maybe because it'll be solidifying that I've not much going on in my life for this presentation to be taking up so much space in it. Like a bleeding placard I'm waving, yeah, that says, "Tech nerd: nothing interesting here. Move along."

A memory surfaces of Brianna at the pub back home. I'd known her all my life, and we'd been dating seriously for several years. Everyone assumed I'd be marrying her. I think I did too.

It was like any other night we spent at the local, but that night she told me she was giving up on me. That made a right bags of it. I panicked and said we could get married, and she rolled her eyes.

"You're beyond understanding," she said.

"Why don't ya tell me?"

She waved a hand at me, as if searching for words. "You're just…empty. You've got no weight to you."

"Weight?"

"Yeah, you're sitting there like a lump, but you're not taking up space here, yeah." And she tapped her fucking heart. "There's not a lot to ya, Conor."

I sat back in my seat, feeling like the lump she's describing.

"I need more, Conor, and you don't have it in ya to be giving it."

And all I could think as I stared at her was, Brianna was knowing me our whole fucking lives, and she felt like I was lacking?

The electricity blinking out brings me back to the present.

"Shit," we both say.

7

WITH THE ELECTRICITY out, we're washing up old school, and Claire's manning the drying towel. We don't have loads, so we make quick work of it. Though it's bucketing outside, we've light enough to see with the drapes open.

Ever since our supermarket trip, I've been hyperconscious of her—where she is, how close she is to me, things like that. Right now her hip is hovering close to me, and I've an insane urge to put this last plate down, reach my hand around her, and tug her body flush to mine. I'm even getting a fine whiff of her scent—clean, feminine, with a citrusy tone, but that last is probably hanging about me too since it's the hotel's shampoo.

All of which adds up to something I never thought would happen—chubby up time doing the washing up. Jaysus. "What is it you might be wanting to do now?" I ask as I carefully hand her that last plate.

"You could give me your presentation." She bumps her hip against mine.

The residue lingering on my skin and on my mind of reliving that moment when my ex-girlfriend and lifelong friend dumped me hangs about. There's a good chance I'll get to know Claire better, and she'll find me lacking too.

Bloody hell. What's it matter if she's discovering I'm a tech nerd and that's about all there is to me? Better for her to be knowing now.

"I'll take a chance on it. Don't be forgetting you asked to hear me present."

"Awesome." Her excitement pushes against me, transforming my anxiety into dread. The presentation can't possibly live up to that.

But like a criminal walking to his execution, I make the steps, slow and dragging, to my laptop and turn it on. She settles herself on the couch, and I sit on the overgrown footstool so she can see the slides on the small screen.

Conor

Finishing the presentation, I stand abruptly, flipping the cover down on my laptop to hide it. A nervous energy is skittering through me, making me want to put some distance between myself and Claire. As if by moving away, I'll dilute the effect of that dry shite presentation.

Unlike how I thought it'd go, she listened intently. And at the end, she gave up some good tips to try. Some of it on the visuals, some of it on my body language and how I was projecting myself. And not once did she give the idea that she was wanting to be elsewhere. The crackling tension between us is still there as well, so that didn't up and disappear as a result.

"So what do you want to be doing now?" I ask as I make myself busy over by the dining table.

Claire reaches over the far end of the couch, which gives me a perfect view of her toned arse underneath her workout shorts. She has no idea what she's doing or how that looks to me.

I'll not be enlightening her.

She's practically draping herself over the couch arm, fine as a cat, her elbows moving. We put a basket there of things to keep us entertained in case the lights went out.

She rises, her face tomato red from being upside down for a few minutes. She holds up the pack of playing cards. "Spit?"

"Are you sure now?" Even though you'll beat my arse.

She sits cross-legged at the end of the couch, her back pressing up against the arm. I settle on the opposite end, and she deals the cards. Unlike at the launderette, the play is a bit more challenging because we keep slapping our cards down, which makes the couch cushions—and the cards—want to go flying.

Soon we're laughing and slapping our hands down as hard as we can, and I'm thinking I haven't felt this *light* in ages.

I gather the cards and deal the next round. "We should've thought to add something to drink to the survival list."

She looks up with a grin. "Hang on." She launches from the couch with such enthusiasm, all the cards slide into the back crease of the couch.

She's back in an instant, holding up an airplane bottle of Jim Beam. "Got this when I thought we were just delayed."

"Just the one?"

"Of course. It was only for me."

I gather the cards into a tight stack and shuffle, the sound of the cards snapping against each other filling the room. "Want to play for it, yeah?"

She settles again on the couch. "What you got in mind?"

I cut the deck. "Hand of poker?"

Her eyes flash with challenge, and damn if that doesn't send some blood south. *Shite.*

"Challenge accepted."

I hop up.

"Where you going?"

I look back at her and wiggle my eyebrows. "If one of us

is winning that lock bottle, I think we need to be doing it up right. With a glass. Savor it like you like to, I'm thinking."

"And ice!" She laughs and waves her hand holding the bottle toward the door, presumably in the direction of the ice machine. "It's starting to get dark. I'll light the candles while you're gone."

While I haven't acquired a taste for ice in my drinks, if that's what she likes, I'll be getting it for her, yeah. I slip on my trainers, grab the ice bucket, and head down the hall. Since the power is out, the ice won't dispense, of course, but I'm hoping it has some kind of lid.

Sure enough, it does. I hold the lid up and scoop the bucket into the mound of ice. This probably violates some health code, but fuck it.

○

CLAIRE

I GET THE candles lit near the couch, their strawberry scent easing into the room and the tiny flame cutting through the twilight settling into the room. Conor's absence also gives me a chance for a pee break.

Also? I need a moment, because when he suggested poker, the words, *make it strip poker*, nearly popped out of my mouth.

I'm not horrified by that impulse. That's not what's making me pause.

What's making me pause is the fact that I…well, *paused*. That's not me. At least that's not the me I strove so hard to become.

I'm the tough girl. One who expresses her wishes.

I wash my hands and dry them, taking my frustration out on the poor white towel. The flashlight on my phone is pointed straight up, as it rests on the counter, but it's enough to see.

The thing is, if it was anyone other than Conor, I'd have said it just to get a reaction out of a male friend. And if it led somewhere, well, it depended on the guy, but I wouldn't say no if it was all in good fun.

So why the damn pause? Some tough girl I am. My interactions with guys are always on my terms, and if they don't like it, they can walk.

I yank open the door and smack into a large, hard, male body. "Ooof."

Conor must have heard the door opening because he's facing my direction. Which means all of my front is intimately pressed against all of *his*.

Oh, um, wow. His free hand settles on my hip, a warm, firm grip. "Chill the beans now there. Didn't mean for you to take a hopper."

God, I love all his expressions. A delicious, demanding heat coils through me, startling me of breath. I stand there stiff, as if contact with this hunk of Irish masculinity has inexplicably flash frozen me.

If I was a chick with a fully paid subscription to the flirt manual, I'd know what to do. Some coy word. Some *signal* that I'm interested.

Wait.

I don't *want* him to know. He can't know. If he learns, and rejects me, I might be tempted to change.

That springs me away from him, all right. And...*smack.* My head hits the door jamb, and I bow forward.

He takes a step so that my head is now pressing to his chest—oh God, his chest—and he cradles my head, rubbing the sore spot. "Jaysus. That had to hurt."

"It does." The gentle touch of his warm hands, his fingers carefully sifting through my hair and massaging my scalp, is starting to ease the sting. Man, that feels *good*.

Which allows me to open my eyes from their screwed-tight position. And notice.

Is that... Is that a *bulge* in his jeans?

"It does hurt," I repeat for some inane reason as that swirling heat from a moment ago narrows into a blazing arrow of need straight to my core.

"Is this helping, yeah?" he asks, his voice low and near my ear, as his fingers continue working their magic on the sting.

"Yes," I breathe as I watch him grow harder.

Seeing his reaction? Knowing there's a better chance I won't be shot down…changes things. And I've wanted him for so long it's getting ridiculous at this point. I mean, I should just go with it, right? I have to believe that my walls are strong enough that I *won't* change into a dang doormat.

And because I *am* that tough girl, I lift my head. "Now. About that poker. Care to make it strip poker?"

8

STRIP POKER?

Her words send a shock wave straight to the semi I've been sporting. The lad jerks, totally on board with the plan. "Are you being serious?" I set the bucket of ice on the kitchen counter.

She pokes me in the chest, her eyes sparking as she looks up at me. Inches from me. "Yes. But let's add some twists to it." She saunters back to the couch. I'm not quite sure how to be reading this situation. Part of me hopes she's meaning what I think she is…

Of course, visions of us later in the game pop into my increasingly fevered imagination. Her sprawling on the couch in just her bra and knickers. And one sock. Why the fuck I'm after imagining one sock on, I have no idea.

It could also be that this is one of those language misfires. Stripping is stripping, though, right?

She plops onto the end of the couch and tucks her legs up. She dangles the bottle of Jim Beam. "We'll still play for this, but since it'll be gone in like two regular shots, we'll add a twist."

"A twist?" I settle on the other end, trying to do it in a way that adjusts the situation down there without being crude about it.

She takes the cards and shuffles them like some Vegas dealer. "Yep, the winner has to take the tiniest sip possible from the mini bottle."

I swallow. "And the loser?"

She breaks the deck of cards and shuffles again. "And the loser has two choices. The first one is you have to confess to something you think is embarrassing. And the second is"—she looks up, a wicked gleam in her eye that I'm liking way too much—"you take off an article of clothing."

Fuck, yeah. Stripping *is* stripping. "Deal."

"We have a deal?"

"Yes. And also…" I nod to her deck of cards. "Deal."

She rolls her eyes and deals.

When the cards are laid out, I suppress a groan. No need to broadcast that I have shite for a hand—numbers and suits all over the place.

I discard two of the biggest outliers and draw. A ten of diamonds and a two of spades. With the ten already in hand, it's the best I'm going to do.

"Okay. What do you have?" she asks.

"A pair."

"I should hope so." She raises an eyebrow and darts a glance to the lad.

I bark out a laugh. "At least they're big." I throw down my tens.

"Ha." She lays down three of a kind. She grins and gives a bounce. "Not big enough."

"You wound me, you do. So how do we pick? Is it the loser doing the choosing or the winner?"

She tilts her head to the side, taking me in. "Let's make it the loser."

Shite. I'd hoped to get a better idea on how this should be playing out by getting her to choose. I decide to be bold.

I rub my hands together and move them to the hem of my T-shirt. Her eyes flare with heat. But I keep moving my hands and slip off one of my trainers, tossing it on the floor where it lands with a dull *thunk*.

She shakes her head. "Lame, Conor."

I shrug. "Gotta be starting somewhere, yeah. Can't go straight to the good stuff now."

She levels me with a get-real stare. "You know I've seen you with your shirt off."

I waggle my brows. "So you looked, did ya?" I don't know where this playful side is coming from. I'm thinking it's this bubble outside of reality we have, free of obligations. Or maybe it's simply Claire.

She just gathers the cards and shoves them my way. "Deal, hot stuff."

"Hot stuff, is it? I like that."

"Deal."

So I deal. She takes the Jim Beam bottle into the kitchen. I twist around and watch. She fishes out a tumbler and fills it with ice, the crunch and clatter of the cubes filling the room. She pours the whole bottle in and returns.

Then she locks her gaze with mine and takes the tiniest sip possible.

For some reason, the sight has me laughing my cacks off. She sets the glass down on the end table, chuckling too.

This time I have the best hand, my pair of Jacks beating her pair of eights. Without ceremony, she removes one of her shoes.

Then I win again. She sticks up her chin. "I have an unreasonable love for the song 'Total Eclipse of the Heart' by Bonnie Tyler."

I snort. "Go on now. You're having me on."

"Nope."

We keep at it, deal after deal, each deciding which to do, having a good laugh the whole time, though there's an edge of tension, which keeps notching up as slowly, piece by piece, we're sitting across from each other on the couch, and she's only wearing her bra and knickers, and I only have my butt-huggers on. Which I'm trying to pretend isn't showing exactly how turned on I fucking am.

So far I've learned that, besides loving Bonnie Tyler, she once was laughing so hard in the common area of her college that she puked up the bright red Gatorade she'd just downed and that she once dove into a pool and emerged without her bikini top, not realizing it had come off.

I've confessed to having my shorts pulled down during a tackle at a packed stadium in Croke Park, Dublin. The Jim Beam is long gone.

Unlike regular strip poker where we have no choice but to take off something we're wearing for a loss, this time it's a choice, and so each time one of us peels off a piece of clothing, it's strangely…revealing. And in more ways than visual. We're choosing to be *going* there.

I'm feeling full of myself when I lay down four of a kind. Will she remove an item of clothing this time? And will it be the bra or knickers…?

My wishful thinking is dashed when she lays down a straight flush with a flourish. "What'll it be, big guy?"

Shite. For some reason, I'm reluctant to find myself bollock naked. Because if I do, I'll no longer be able to keep pretending that I don't have a raging hard-on and bluer balls than a bleeding Smurf. She's bound to notice. In fact, she just did because when she thinks I'm not looking, she flicks her gaze there and quickly away, and scarlet dots her cheeks.

So I blurt out, "My long-term girlfriend in Ireland dumped me."

What the bloody hell? And cue *this* moment as ripe for confessing as leaving myself bloody mortified.

Her eyes round. But she just shakes her head. "Well, she was an idiot."

I laugh, because what else will I be doing otherwise? I gather up the cards and deal again. This time she loses.

I'm dreading her saying something just as terrible, because somehow it would feel as if she were trying to smooth things over by making things "even." But it wouldn't. It would leave myself feeling mollycoddled.

But she surprises me. She looks up, and without ceremony,

her arms twine to her back, pushing her chest forward, and unhook her plain white bra. Which I've been valiantly trying to ignore how well they hold up her perky breasts.

The bra sags, and those breasts… Oh, they spring free, open to the air. And to my gaze.

I can't help it. I'm a guy. I stare.

And swallow.

My hands flex on the deck of cards I was in the middle of gathering, bending them. I drop the cards, spraying them across the couch cushion.

Smooth, Conor.

As I stare, the tips begin to… Fuck me, they begin to harden, don't they?

My breathing gets a little uneven, and I glance back up to her face, searching her eyes. She's searching mine too, her gaze fierce with defiance, but with a hint of vulnerability, as well as indecision.

Decision apparently made, she leans closer.

My breath hitches, and I swear to Mother Mary, Joseph, and Jesus on the feckin' cross, every nerve ending on my skin comes alive in anticipation. I lean closer.

She whispers, "Deal the cards." And flicks a wicked glance down at my growing erection.

Fuuuck.

I blow out a breath and lean myself back. I gather up the cards, all the while telling my dick to stand down.

I guarantee you, I've gone thick as a plank, since all my blood is hurtling south. So, yeah, I lose the next hand. Frankly, the last few minutes become a haze for me.

So when I lose, I look up.

Her gaze is challenging.

I could confess to another embarrassing thing.

Or, I could take off my butt-huggers.

I take off my butt-huggers.

And I can't help but notice that she looks as if she's holding her breath.

9

CLAIRE

MY GAZE IS glued to Conor's long fingers as he catches them on the elastic waist of his boxers and tugs downward. My blood is thrashing its beats so hard, it almost matches the tempo of the rain beating down outside. All through the game, it was a challenge not to notice his growing erection. Each time he opted to remove an article of clothing, I felt a flare of triumph.

I have no idea what I'm doing, but it seems to be working, and I'm gonna keep going with what I'm doing.

The fabric catches on the tip of his cock, and Conor eases it over and shoves it down his muscular thighs, tossing it onto the floor to join the other pieces of our clothing.

I pull in a shuddering breath.

Whoa. I can't...I can't even begin to describe how he looks right now. At this moment. But I'm going to try. Because—holy wow. He's magnificent. His broad shoulders, the biceps a perfect curve, block my view of the kitchen. The candlelight casts shadows across his skin, making smoky gray shapes dance and flicker across his chest as if it enjoys playing across its surface. Like I want to.

Then there's the nicely delineated pecs, with a sprinkling of dark red hair decorating their smooth planes and marching down the bumps of his abs to…yeah, wow, the proudest and *largest* cock I've ever seen. Boy, am I not kidding.

It jerks a little as if my staring has caught its attention. Shit.

I'm staring.

I dart my gaze back to his, and he's staring too. At me. With eyes that are hooded. And filled with desire.

For me.

Holy shit. Heat rushes across my skin, and a zing happens down in my girly parts.

But it's clear he's letting me control what's going to happen between the two of us, which I really, really appreciate.

I can do this. I can have casual sex with him and *not* get all…emotional. Walls in place? Check. I snap the metaphorical elastic on my big girl panties and edge forward on the couch. "Can I touch you?"

He pulls in a shuddering breath, the action tightening his muscles all over. "Please, yeah."

Thick, eager anticipation swirls in the air between us as I reach forward and touch the tip, velvet smooth and warm. His whole body tenses, and a low moan escapes that he quickly swallows.

God, that's sexy.

I circle my fingers around his shaft and skim them down and back up, barely touching the hot, silky skin. Like my fingers are mapping the contours.

Then I give a little squeeze, and his hand shoots out and holds my wrist.

"Claire," he chokes out.

I look up at him. "Yes?" My breaths are shallow.

He swallows and looks into my eyes. "What is it you'd be wanting?" His voice is low, and it holds so much in those words—anticipation, trepidation, need, heat. The low pitch, the cadence, the words, and the meaning riding them, they all seep inside, giving me my answer.

What do I want? "You."

It's as if I lit the fuse to a bomb that just hit its payload, because he launches forward, pushing me back against the couch. My breath leaves me in a rush. His whole body covers mine, the soft nap of the couch fabric a cool embrace against the skin of my back. The playing cards crinkle beneath me.

Holy shit. This reaction. It's for *me*.

His mouth crashes into mine, feverish, and all other sensation flees except the magnificent feel of his lips crushing mine, hot, urgent. If I ever even allowed myself the fantasy of imagining our first kiss, I would have guessed it'd be like this—up front, impatient, rough. Our mouths are taking swipes at each other, and I fist my hands in that luscious red hair of his to try to hold his head still, to get the right angle. Which works, and our tongues tangle. The taste of him—carnality laced with bourbon—bursts along my taste buds, lighting me up, and I soak it in. Swirling heat blooms in my chest and arrows down, pooling in my sex.

Our breaths are coming fast, our frantic mouth tango making it difficult to catch air. I want to be on top, though. Not that I don't like the delicious feel of him stretched out over me. Believe me, I do—boy, do I—but I want to direct this, especially if it's my only chance to be with him.

We girls have needs too, and in my experience, this is the only way I can be sure they're met. And, yeah, I want them met. With him. I glance sideways—there's enough gap between the couch and the oversized, footrest-slash-coffee table. I pinch his side.

"Roll," I gasp against his lips.

He jerks in surprise, holding himself up by his elbow. Which gives me room and leverage to lock my legs around his and roll us both off the couch.

He lands on the carpet with a startled *oof*, me splayed across all that delicious, hard muscle that makes up Conor's gorgeous body. I rise up and adjust myself against his hard girth. Outside the window, which I have a clear view of, the world is gray, rain lashing like ropes against the window. I'm still sporting my boring white panties, but his thickness, and his heat, is pressing hard against my core right through the cotton. Gawd.

I rock forward and back, smoothing my hands along his work-of-art chest, his tiny hairs tickling across my palms. His strong, broad hands fly to my waist and brush up my stomach until he's cupping my boobs.

He flicks a thumb against both. And that heady heat shoots through me again, from my nipples down to where I'm starting to ache for him.

I gasp and arch forward, giving him better access for the boob-flicking, because OMG. He caresses and circles the tips, working them into tight, hardened points. And boy, does that do it for me. I scrape my nails across his nipples, and he bucks under me.

Then his hot hands are back at my waist, his grip sure and strong, and he's dragging me up, my core rubbing deliciously across his hard abs on its short journey.

Conor's eyes are hooded and glazed with lust. When he's pulled me close enough, he latches his mouth around a nipple and sucks hard. I jerk against him, as if zapped by electricity. Heat rockets through me, flushing my skin.

Shit. Wow. This reaction is unusual for me. Usually I just feel a pleasant hum. If I'm lucky. Sometimes I don't feel much of anything at all, except a desire to please. But this? I'm like a live wire that he's playing with, and I'm just a jerky ball of need. And want.

And I *ache*.

Who *is* this person?

If most people feel this all the time when they have sex, no wonder everyone's always after some.

He pulls away, then curls his tongue out and flicks my other nipple, and I'm squirming, aching for him to tug and suck, not tease. But he keeps flicking and circling, which winds me up, yes, but also isn't quite enough. And he knows it. I can see the battle in his gaze—wanting to tease me to draw out my pleasure but also wanting to give us what we both want. Now.

Then he flips us over, bumping us against the cushioning

of the overgrown footrest. His eyes are pools of heat and want, and I'm sure I'm reflecting back the same.

"Conor," I whisper.

Fuck, I want this guy bad. Always have. Maybe that's why other guys haven't really turned my crank—they weren't *him*.

He shifts to the side, his free hand skimming down my stomach. His hooded gaze follows his exploring hand, as if feel is not enough—he has to *see* too. The rough tip of a finger circles the skin around my belly button, and then he trails his fingers down my skin. All the tiny hairs over every inch of my skin, I swear to God, are now standing at attention. My breath catches and releases.

His fingers bump into the elastic of my panties. Skim back and forth, tracing the bare, sensitized skin bordering the edge, and it's as if all that skin is brand-spanking new, feeling touch for the first time. His touch.

His gaze flips to mine. Even though I was pretty clear with the *I want you* thing, he seems to be checking in again. Which I appreciate. Which makes him all the hotter.

"Please," I gasp.

His eyes flare, and he edges those warm fingers under the elastic, skimming, brushing. He probes through my trim curls until he reaches where I'm dying for him. His focus returns to his hand, and I watch—fascinated—as his arm muscles bunch and flex with the motions of his fingers. He gently plays with my clit, teasing it into a plumper, harder nub, and now I'm thrashing my legs, cuz *Jeez*.

Then—oh—he dips a blunt finger down and presses it inside, just a tad, finding me wet, and back up to my clit, slicking the evidence of my arousal around my swollen nub.

I shudder. "Conor."

"Ah Jaysus, you're so beautiful," he rasps. "Feckin' gorgeous."

"More." I arch against his hand. "Harder."

He obliges, circling my clit and dipping, adding two fingers on the next venture.

I'm restless, and I want. But in order for me to be tough, I have to also be in control, and while I'm enjoying his ministrations, it's making me panic and second guess myself.

And since he's on his side, balancing the whole of his weight on an elbow, I'm easily able to flip him onto his back.

He chuckles and grasps my waist. "I was just getting started, yeah."

"And now I want to get started." I smile and ease down his body, and his eyes widen, hope and heat flaring in them.

10

CLAIRE

ONE OF CONOR'S hands clutches my shoulder, holding on, but the other slaps the edge of the couch as I edge down his body, my lips brushing down his torso. His fingers curl around the cushion and grip, as if he's gotta hold on. Playing cards cascade down and bounce onto the floor.

The scent of our arousal fills the room, mixing with the strawberry aroma of the candles. And because the power outage knocked out the A/C, a light sheen of sweat films our flushed skin.

When my lips reach his belly button, I graze it with the flat of my tongue. His whole body tenses.

But his grip remains on my shoulder and the couch, and he doesn't push.

I trace one of the V's angling down to his magnificent package. And then along the other seam. He tastes clean and salty and delicious. Mmmm. I take a moment to savor the flavors on my tongue.

God, whenever he was shirtless on the field and reached up to stretch, or run his hand through his hair, I saw this V, and I was always dying, *dying*, to do this. Lick it. Learn the different flavors of his skin on my tongue. Explore where it led. And now... I'm doing it.

His engorged cock lies heavy against his stomach, as if the V perfectly frames it.

I touch my tongue to the thick base and lave up its length to the tip. He pushes up his hips, his ab muscles tightening with the movement and his tension.

"Fuck, loveen," he gasps.

I lick the hood and then along the crease, lapping up the pre-cum. I cradle his balls, playing their delicate weight between my fingers, and then grip the base of his cock. I watch his reactions, adjusting my grip, and tug. He's more sensitive than I'm used to—the slightest pressure makes him curse and tense and shudder.

Jesus, that's hot as hell. My core clenches, aching for his fullness. I shift, lift his cock, and swallow the first inch and suck back up. Normally, I don't find giving head enjoyable—it's just something I do to please my bed partner. I might like to be in control, but I'm not selfish with my bed partners. And while that's all well and good, it doesn't usually turn *me* on.

Until now. And it's clear from his reactions that he's enjoying it. I discover a rhythm with my hand and mouth that elicits the most vocal reaction—the word "fuck" coming out on a soft grunt every time I suck back up to the tip.

And for the first time, I find myself wanting to make him come in my mouth. Normally, I don't let that happen.

On the next suck, my mouth is suddenly empty of him. What—?

I'm airborne. Conor's hands are clamped around my waist, dragging me up, and I slap my palms against the soft nap of the carpet to get balance. He arches up and hungrily starts kissing the hell out of me. I'm kinda draped randomly against him, so I readjust until I'm gliding my core up and down his length, the wetness from my mouth and from my panties quickly soaking the fabric. The rhythm matches the mating of our tongues.

Unable to wait any longer to feel him against me, I rest my weight on one hand, lift up, and grab the elastic of my underwear. But before I can remove them, his hand is there, and he grips the fabric. He tugs, jerking my hips to the side. He grunts, yanks again, and a tearing sound fills the room.

Holy shit. He just ripped my panties off.

I thought that only happened in books.

"Tell me you have a condom," I ask.

"Yeah. Rucksack. Side pocket. Inside an Altoids tin."

I push upward and slap around behind me. A hand cups my breast, and I'm patting around more urgently. I spy a dark pile of clothing on top of his duffel, and I drag it toward me. I shove the clothes off and search in his side pocket.

All the while, his hands are busy massaging my breasts or pressing against my clit and circling. Which is making my body shake and vibrate and my search harder.

Where is—? I pull the duffel onto his belly, blocking his access to me.

"Whatcha!" he grumps.

"You want to get it on, don't you?"

"Fuck, yeah."

I laugh. "Then patience, big boy."

I snag the tin and shove the duffel to the side. He grabs it from my hands, flicks it open, and pulls out a foil. He rips it open and fishes out the condom. I move my hips to free him, but I also snatch the condom away.

I want to roll it on myself.

"You like taking charge, do you now?" he says on a laugh.

I don't answer, I'm too focused on my goal: sheathing his hard girth. And getting him inside me.

When he's completely covered—God, he's huge—I brace my hands on his muscular chest. I look up at him.

"Ready?"

"C'mere to me," he groans.

He grabs hold of himself, and I let the fat tip edge inside. We both tense and pull in a sharp breath.

With how much the crown is stretching me, it confirms that he's going to be the biggest guy I've ever taken inside me. A dull ache pounds there, screaming to allow his hot length to spread me wide, to feel all of him inside me.

But I want to control this encounter. It's the first, and maybe the only time, I'll feel Conor fill me. All this masculine hotness. And even if somehow we do this again, this will always be the first time.

And so I don't want to rush. I want to feel his texture, feel his heat, feel the stretch, feel him fully seated.

It's like my first bites of food when I sit down for a meal. I want to savor it. Savor *him*.

I shudder and push down an inch, and holy fucking God, the exquisite molten slide is *whoa*. My inner muscles contract and relax, trying to accommodate him, and the stretch is almost painful. Almost. And so it's also so *so* delicious.

Conor's head is thrown back, his neck muscles stretching, his biceps bunching and flexing as he grips my hips, his fingers digging into me, but restraining from pushing me down fully like he obviously wants to.

I drag upward, the friction making me tremble. The truth is, he's so huge, I need adjustment time, but God, the friction is making me antsy, the ache inside now a greedy throb.

I suck in a deep breath, readjust my knees, and just go for it. I impale myself fully down, and he bows upward. "Fuck!"

I still, gasping sharply. His hands dive into my hair, and he's kissing me as I feel him thicken. I still can't move because, ohmygod, but the sensation of him seated fully inside me is unlike anything I've ever felt.

The hollow ache that was waiting to be filled is not satisfied—it's now urging me to *move*. I grip his shoulders, and, still kissing, I slide up and back down. He groans into my mouth.

Soon my movements are so frantic we can't kiss anymore without injury, and I throw my head back, all of my consciousness zeroed in on how he feels inside and against me—the heat, the friction.

Holy shit. A rare, sex-induced orgasm barrels toward me, making me desperate to grab it.

But before it can overtake me, he pushes me onto my

back. Pulls out, and thrusts back into me.

"Yes!" But damn, I hope that wasn't my last chance at that orgasm. An orgasm with *Conor.*

I grip his athletic ass—God, he has such a firm ass—and urge him deeper on each thrust.

On the next plunge, he arches up, whips his arms behind him, and grabs my wrists. The strength required to basically do a plank above me? Whoa.

Inside me, his girth is hot and thick, my blood pounding in my ears and in my clit. He puts my hands over my head, holding them both in one of his, while his other arm draws up one of my legs, looping it over his forearm.

"Holy shit," I gasp as he drags out and slams inside me even deeper. He pounds into me, and even though he has my wrists constrained above my head, I'm so lost in the feeling of him moving inside me, I don't care that he's taken control.

All the while, his mouth is ranging over every inch of skin he can reach, pattering me with kisses and tiny bites and curses.

That orgasm that was just out of reach before, the one I was desperately chasing because of its rarity, blasts through me with no warning, the tug and bliss and heat so powerful, I actually scream out his name.

I'm jerking, the aftershocks causing me to buck and writhe against him. He releases my wrists, thank God, and I latch them around his torso and hold on as he drives into me with more urgency.

And…whoa another orgasm builds. Am I a greedy person for wanting it too before he finds his pleasure?

I've never had a double orgasm from sex.

I grab his ass, urging him onward, greedily grinding him into me. He shifts the angle of his hips, rising partway up but somehow making his pubic bone press against me with each thrust. His whole body is one giant hunk of tension and muscle and maleness as he pumps into me. He does a little twist of his hips, and that gluttonous part of me is like *fuck yes*, because I explode in another searing orgasm.

Holyshitholyshitholyshit.

He thrusts inside once more, holds still, and because I'm like a stretched glove around his thick hardness, I can feel him kick inside me with his release.

Oh wow.

He drags out slightly, pushes in again, and I clamp down on him tightly, my body still wracked with aftershocks. He collapses on top of me shuddering, his breaths sawing in and out near my ear. Mine is too. Our hearts are beating so hard, I can feel its thumps everywhere we're touching. Every. Where. Even deep inside.

We're slick with sweat, and I'm holding on to him tight, my mind blissed out as I slowly piece myself back together.

Holy shit.

What *was* that?

Oh, just hot-as-sin sex with fucking Conor McDaid. I skim my hands all over his slick skin and try to get my breathing under control. Outside, it's prematurely dark from the storm, the rain drubbing against the windows in spurts, as if being thrown against it over and over. The candles are still alight, their flickering shadows playing across the ceiling.

"I must be crushing you," he groans.

He rolls to the side, taking me with him. I let him and snuggle up against his chest, unwilling to leave the moment. Because when I do, reality will return, and I really, *really* love this unreality.

Wow.

My breathing calms, and I keep my head on his chest, savoring this moment until it inevitably ends.

11

CLAIRE

WE'RE MOSTLY COOLED off, though the room's still muggy from lack of A/C and our, er, exertions. Our heart rates have returned to normal, and it's…nice. *Good* nice. We're comfortable, and we're not feeling awkward. At least, I'm not.

A ringing sound jolts us.

Conor groans. "My mobile is bleeding after me."

"Can you let it ring?"

"That's the tone for work."

The way he says it, I know he can't let it go to voice mail, so I ease off him. He levers up and snatches his jeans, fishing out his phone.

"Yeah?"

His body stiffens. He stands and strolls to the kitchen, holding the phone to his ear and listening to whatever bad news he's getting. He's not saying anything, but his body language says it's not good.

His hand tunnels into his dark red hair and clenches.

"And wasn't I telling Steven himself that code needed looking at again. Too many bugs showing up in the initial testing of it." His accent thickens as his frustration mounts.

Another pause.

"Yeah. I'm on it."

He ends the call. "Fucking hell. Ain't that a savage dose." He marches into the bathroom, and the toilet flushes. He comes back out sans-condom and calls someone else.

I'm feeling exposed, lying on the floor. The post-coital buzz has definitely packed up and vamoosed.

Since it's evening, I pad into the bathroom and clean my face and brush my teeth. Then I don my sleepwear, the fresh scent of the detergent we used today filling my nose as I pull the T-shirt on over my head.

Holy shit. It hits me. I just had sex with Conor McDaid. Hot, sweaty, oh-my-God sex.

In a way, the interruption is a blessing—it doesn't let me read into it more than what it is. A hookup.

As I'm having a mild freak-out, he's pacing in the living room in all his naked glory, but he's in full Alpha mode, making one phone call after another, barking out orders, giving some a hard time, others he's apologizing for the unexpected problem, whatever it is. It's all tech speak.

I locate my tablet and stay in my bedroom to give him a semblance of privacy, but I can't focus on one word of the ebook I'm currently reading. He marches back and forth and so becomes visible through the doorway for a brief moment, and I keep looking up, as if my body has an internal timer tuned to when he'll appear.

I'm struck by the change in him. He's back to his non-smiling self, and it's a weird juxtaposition. This guy pacing in the living room—all take-charge and serious—is not the flirting, carefree man who was just inside me. This guy…this guy feels like a stranger.

A flutter of panic builds in my chest at how take-charge he is. How *good* he is at it.

Then I catch myself—because that doesn't matter. We're just having fun while stuck together during a storm, and while he's fulfilling every fantasy I had about him, I need to remember that this won't work—*we* won't work—when we return home.

Before, when he was my secret crush, it was easy for me

to be smug about my strength. It wasn't being tested.

But now that I've been with him? And it was the hottest sex I've ever had? How can I keep my walls intact if we actually *date*? I'll get attached. I'll want to morph to please him. I'll want *everything*.

○

CONOR

WHAT A BLEEDING mess.

I left the coding team in good shape for the next phase of testing the new app. I met with each team member, set expectations, deliverables, fucking deadlines, and made contingency plans.

Then Steven drove it arseways by doing a piss-poor review of the code segment he was in charge of.

I hang up from the last call.

I find myself in a hotel room, naked, staring at a darkened window as rain is pissing against the glass pane. And it takes me a second to zero in on where I am and why I'm feckin' naked.

Then I remember.

And just like that, I'm back into myself fully and glance frantically around. "Claire?"

"In here!"

I step into my jeans and lean into the bedroom. She's stretched out on her stomach, her feet in the air, crossed. A tablet rests on the bed in front of her, its glow illuminating her face. Feckin' hell. Sex with Claire was deadly. She's looking mighty feen, hair still mussed from the riding. And while, of course, my lad's piping up for another go, I'm also feeling the frustration with work ebb away just looking at her.

"Could you eat now?"

She glances up and makes to rise. "Sure. Lemme help."

"You stay there. I want to be doing this, yeah." She gives me a big grin that goes right inside me, it does. I hustle to the kitchen and busy myself making a hodge-podge of a dinner out of the non-perishables we'd bought. I'm halfway through when my poxy mobile dings again.

I pick it up—it's a text alert. One that's triggered whenever my sister is late for a payment. Frustration spikes through me. I hit the icon for Siobhan.

"Hey."

"We talked earlier." She's sounding groggy. "Why are you ringing now?"

I pull my mobile away and look at the time. *Shite*. The time difference slipped my mind. "You didn't tell me you were three days late with the mortgage."

"What are you at, Conor, ragging at me?" Her voice definitely sounds awake now.

"How many times is it I've told you, I can help you when you're needing it. If you were short a few quid, why didn't ya tell me?"

Her breath pushes into the speaker. "You don't need to be sending me anything at all. The farm's mine, remember? It's mine to handle."

"Then why aren't the bills paid off, yeah?"

She's quiet for a moment—probably picturing all the ways she can belt me from across the pond. "Not that you'd know much about it, but I've bought a ram from over near Ballinasloe. A fine lad, big as an ass, which is what you're being. And I've got two old ewes to market for their meat come the morrow. I'll have the payment made soon enough."

"You shouldn't—"

"Conor. It's past time to start believing I can handle the farm without you, yeah?"

Agitation and frustration rise within me. I'm *wanting* to help. If she's not letting me put a finger in it, what am I good for? Leaves me a right bowsie. If I hadn't left her, she wouldn't be shouldering all the burden herself.

"Night, Conor. Let me try to get in some sleep?"

"You know I'm only looking out for yourself, yeah?"

She groans. "Sure look it, and being a right gowl about it."

Shite. I hang up and finish prepping dinner. Then I find myself setting the table for the meal, because I know that's what Claire's liking.

No. Scratch that. That's only partly true. It's growing on me as well, because when we sat down earlier and took our time eating, it weren't half bad. The feeling of sharing a moment together. Not rushing. Enjoying.

That frantic call from work was a sharp reminder that I put my whole self too much into a soulless corporation. Rushing to get ahead there. Rushing through my life.

So stopping and enjoying? Yeah, I'm finding I like it. Maybe too much.

Claire

"DINNER'S ON," CONOR calls from the kitchen.

I power down my tablet to conserve the battery and step into the main room.

He's set the table.

A part inside me goes squishy at that. Especially when I notice a couple of candles glowing in the center. I *know* the candles are because we need to see, but I can't help thinking it looks romantic, okay? Like it means something.

"Wow, this looks great. Thank you."

I settle at the table and drape my napkin across my lap. He's made some kind of sandwich with—I lift the top slice of bread. "Canned ham and potato chips?"

"And sugar, mind."

"Ooookay." I take a bite. Different. But surprisingly good.

The flavors mix and dance on my tongue, and I close my eyes. Mmmmm.

I open them, ready to tell Conor thank you again, but he's staring at me with hooded eyes. He's still bare-chested, though he put his jeans back on.

"What?"

"Never thought watching someone eat would turn me on," he says, voice low with a trace of surprise.

Warmth blooms in my chest. "Oh yeah?" I take another bite, this time taking my time biting into it, closing my eyes, and giving a good "Mmmm."

He closes his eyes and groans.

He's distracted and edgy, but he's joking with me, interacting, so I know the edginess isn't about us. There's no awkwardness in the air, or regret.

I take another bite. "What's going on?"

He starts eating and, in between bites, tells me about his sister buying a ram and delaying her loan payment.

When he's done, I say, "You're worried." It's clear he doesn't believe his sister can take care of the farm and its needs.

"Of course I'm worried. She could lose everything she's been working her arse off to keep."

"It's her farm to lose, isn't it?"

He falls back against his chair. "But if I hadn't left—" He breaks off and looks to the side. Guilt wafts from him, so thick I can feel it.

"But you did. And she elected to take on the responsibility."

He leans forward, eyes intent on me. "And I can be helping her with that. But she won't see her way clear to it."

Something else is at work. Something he might not even be aware of.

"Has she asked for help in the past?" I'm trying to figure out why he feels like he has to help. If she fell into some trouble before and he bailed her out…

"No."

"So she's never needed your help?"

His jaw clenches, and he glances away. "No. Hasn't once asked me for help. And I'm clear over here. If I can't be there mending fences for her, or helping with the feeding or any of the other physical chores, it's the least I could be doing, yeah, to be sending her money."

Siobhan seems as if she's doing fine, and Conor has engaged Brother Mode a bit too hard.

"You like to help. She's lucky to have a brother looking out for her." I didn't mean to reveal anything with that statement, but he looks at me sharply.

His eyes wander my face. "You have a brother or sister or two?"

I push the last bite to the side of my plate. "No. I sometimes do wonder what it would have been like to have one." And when that happens, I quickly snuff that thought, because most likely the sibling would have steamrolled over me too, or tried to micromanage like Conor's doing with his sister.

But maybe it might have played out differently with me. What if I had a sibling who was supportive but not take-charge. Would my life be different now?

It's rare that I take a trip down pity lane, but I allow a tiny fantasy of having a brother or sister who was there for me when my life fell apart. Hell, a sibling who would have helped me see the danger sooner. Or at the very least, wanted to help me rebuild when I left Mom and Pensacola. I'd have still turned away any financial assistance and worked the two jobs to put myself through the local community college in Sarasota, but it would have been nice to know that security net was there.

To have someone familiar by my side during that scary-because-I-could-mess-up time.

CONOR

I HELP CLAIRE clear the table, and we take up our spots by the sink for washing up.

But as I'm drying plates—she took up wash duty this time—I find I'm on edge about her questions regarding the farm and Siobhan. I'm not upset at Claire, and that's what's got me on edge. I don't know *what* is bothering me about it.

I shove that aside and put away the first plate. The domesticity feels odd, but also…nice. I'm not used to this sharing or taking time out of the day to savor a meal.

It makes me wonder…what if we continued this when we return to Sarasota? She has me wanting to know more about her.

It could get awkward since we're both in the same league, but I'm starting to see that opening up to someone isn't necessarily a bad thing.

Maybe that's what's got me on edge? That I'm not balking at opening up?

12

CLAIRE

WE'RE QUIET AS we put away the dishes, but it's a contemplative quiet, not an awkward one.

I hand the last glass to Conor, and my phone rings. I dig it out from where it had fallen in the seat cushions and glance at the screen. A number I don't recognize.

"Hello?" Normally I don't answer a strange number, but with the weather emergency, I make an exception. I'm ready to hang up, though, if it's a telemarketer.

"Claire Hitchins?"

"Yes. Can I help you?"

"This is the nurse on call at Saint Joseph Hospital in Denver."

Denver?

The nurse continues, "You're listed as the emergency contact for Constance Hitchins."

My stomach evaporates as cold sweat pops onto my skin. "She's my mom. Is she okay?" Panic and worry have made my voice higher, and it cracks on the last word. Yeah, I had to cut her from my life to protect myself, but she's still my mom and I don't want her to be hurt.

But what is she doing in *Denver*?

"She's stable," the nurse announces with practiced calm.

"She was in a car accident and was taken to the ER. She was admitted to ICU and was just transferred to a ward. She should be released by the end of the week. We tried reaching you earlier but couldn't get through."

My chest eases a fraction. "Thank you," I whisper, my relief stealing the volume from my words.

"Do you want her room number?"

"Oh. Yes. Hang on." I dash into my room and grab the pad of paper and pen from the hotel. "Okay, I'm ready."

I take down the information and thank the nurse. I'm not sure how long I stand there after hanging up, but my hands are shaking, the pen still tight in my grip. I collapse onto the bed, my knees weak. Then guilt floods me anew when I realize that I'm not immediately making plans to go see her. She's in the friggin' hospital, yet my mind didn't go straight to logistics.

I tell myself that I cut her from my life for a reason and that reason hasn't changed.

The bed shifts, and Conor's strong hands are gripping mine, which are still shaking. "You've gone white. What's the story with your mam?" Conor's voice pulls me into focus.

"She's been in a car accident."

He squeezes my hands. "Shite. How bad is it?"

I stand up and move to the window, though I can't see anything beyond them. "They say she's stable and should be released by the end of the week. The storm must have knocked out the cell service for a bit because they tried to call me earlier."

"Fuck. And here you are stuck in Atlanta without a way to be seeing her."

I look out the window. That guilt is now like a knife, cutting up my throat.

"Yeah. Too bad," I manage to say, throat tight.

"Maybe the weather will clear soon, and you can still fly there. Or rent a car and drive." He closes the distance between us in two strides and takes my hands again, turning me to face him. Mine feel like cold lumps. "Where is she keeping herself?"

"Denver," I croak.

"That'd be one hell of a road trip, yeah." He picks up his cell. "Let me ring some folks."

Panic hits me, and I pace into the kitchen and back. "Who?"

He looks up from scrolling around the screen. "The airport. Delta. Maybe we can find out when they'll be getting clearance to fly again. At least then you'll know when you'll be likely to leave."

I snatch the phone from his hand, and he startles.

My palm feels sweaty holding it in my tight grip. "I don't need you to do that."

His forehead pulls down in a frown. "And why would you not be needing it?"

"Because…" I swallow and take a deep breath. "Because I'm not planning to fly out there," I finish on a rush.

He stands there staring at me. Then blinks. "Your mother's bloody banjaxed her car and herself, and you're not wanting to visit?"

I flinch and turn away, not wanting to look at his face as he judges me. "No."

"But ya have ta be goin'." His accent has grown thicker. "Who else will be sittin' with herself?"

"I can't. You don't understand."

The urge to spill and admit to him how sick and weak I used to be is pushing against me.

But this is just a fling. You don't go dumping emotional crap like that on a fling. No matter how sweet that fling is being. I spin back to the window.

He steps around until he's in front of me again. He leans to the side until he can look up into my face. "You're talking rubbish now. Let me do what I can to help."

Even while I'm getting increasingly frustrated and angry that he's pushing me on this, my heart breaks a little at that statement. He always wants to help.

I shake my head. "You can't fix this. It's my decision.

My problem."

"Yeah, but—"

I hold up a hand and face him. Realizing that my excuses sound lame and that I look weak for not going, I say, "I'll think about it."

Anything to end this discussion.

○

Conor

It's clear that Claire doesn't want to talk about what's happening with her mam. Biggest clue? She's now in her room reading on her tablet. I run my hands through my hair.

Her mam's in fucking hospital, and she won't be trying to see her?

I'm more agitated about it than she is, and I don't even know her mother from Adam.

When I kick the dark red footstool, I'm realizing something else—I'm bleeding pissed off. And resenting what she's throwing away.

It's an ugly set of emotions, I know.

My mother didn't have much love or care for me or Siobhan. Not enough to stick around. She walked out on us when I was fucking seven. *Seven.* And if there's a chance her mam has any care for Claire, she needs to be heading to Denver. I've seen and met enough mothers to know mine was not the usual stripe.

I fall back into the couch with a sigh and cross my arms. The other part that's hurting my heart? I opened up to her about the farm when she questioned me, but when I'm asking what's troubling *her*? Instant dry up.

I'd have to be thick not to see there's something she's not telling me.

Claire pops back out of the room fully dressed. "I'm getting stir crazy. Wanna go watch the storm from the lobby?"

I look at her for a moment and will my emotions to bite the back of my bollocks. A lot of these emotions are because of my *own* past. That's not fair to her. I nod and blow out a breath, releasing some tension. "Sure, yeah. Let me pull on my trainers."

She blows out the candles, and soon we're padding down the hall. Eerie red bulbs pulse along the hallway enough to leave anyone with sense feeling their hairs rise. We must not be the only guests after getting ourselves a bit stir crazy, because when we get to the foyer, it's jammers with a good-sized crowd hanging about. Most of them look to be business men and women types, looking out-of-place in "casual" clothes. It probably doesn't help that the whole scene looks strange—the hotel's set up lamps on tripods hooked to a rattling generator, lighting the place up like a movie set.

Because I hate how we left things, I slip my fingers into hers as we walk to the big picture window. She stiffens for a moment and then squeezes my hand, making my heart feel warm, yeah. Generator-run lights are arrayed out front, giving us a better view of what's going on outside than we could get from our room. The Bradford pears are at a near forty-five degree angle in the parking lot.

Rain is still bucketing against the panes.

Nearby, some boyo has a weather radio plugged into a power line running from the generator.

"What's the news?" I ask.

He looks up. "The eye passed east of here about an hour ago."

"So we didn't get a letup," Claire adds.

"Nope. Hurricane hit Atlanta just after it was downgraded from a Category 2 to a 1, so we're seeing winds around ninety miles an hour."

"Jaysus."

"Yeah, they think we'll be out from under its arms by early morning."

I nod. "Thanks for the update, yeah."

"Sure thing."

We watch the wind playing about for a time. The rain's sounding like tiny beads hitting the glass over and over.

Claire rests her head on my upper arm. Just that tiny gesture has me feeling like I won a major victory with her. A strange notion after what we were doing on the hotel floor, but some gestures can just feel more intimate somehow.

"Seeing Mother Nature like this can really make you feel insignificant," she says.

I squeeze her hand. "Sure it can."

Behind us a guitar chord strums. Claire tugs on my hand, and we make our way over to a corner of the common area where two lads are having a go at playing covers on their acoustic guitars.

The couches and chairs in front of the duo are taken, but there's a spot on the arm of one of the couches so I settle there and pull Claire onto my lap. It feels great having this excuse to hold her against myself. I may be turning into a sap, but fuck it.

The lads are playing a cover of a Nine Inch Nails song. Their voices are good, and their playing's not half middling. Everyone claps when they finish, and they go right into another tune. It's obvious they've played a lot together—they have that casual ease with each other of best mates.

At the end of the next song, a cover of "Black Horse and the Cherry Tree," someone calls out "Stairway to Free Bird," and we all obligingly laugh at the stale joke. But they do glance up, and the darker haired one asks, "Any requests?"

Soon we're all laughing and singing along to different tunes. It reminds me of good times at the local pub back home, and homesickness bleeds into me. In Ireland, the lads never batted an eye about singing whenever the bunch of us gathered and needed to be entertaining ourselves.

My first time at a pub in the States with some other ex-pats, we drew some stares when we broke out into song. Americans can be good *craic*, but it's in a different way.

By now my arms are completely encircling Claire's waist, snugging her up against my chest, my chin on her shoulder as we finish singing a Simon and Garfunkel song. Talk about an oldie but goodie.

I turn my face into her neck, inhaling her scent and pressing my lips just below the ear. She shivers.

I whisper, "Ready to call it a night, yeah?"

She turns in my lap and looks at me, her eyes searching. She gives me a sensual, but safe for the kiddies, kiss. "Yes."

13

I FOLLOW CLOSE behind Claire, watching her backside sway, as we say our goodbyes to the closest hotel guests and head to our room.

I dig the keycard from my back pocket and swipe us in.

I've just cleared the door, Claire in front of me, when she whirls around and shoves me against the door. Fierce determination lights her eyes. Fuck. She's pissed off about something, I'm thinking, but then her hands are in my hair and she's kissing me hard enough to be wearing my face off.

Much better than fighting.

Our tongues are tangling, heating me up. I clasp my hands at her waist and switch positions, pushing herself up against the wall. Her kisses grow more frantic, and she hops up, whipping her legs around my waist.

I manage to tear my mouth away to say, "We have ourselves a bed, yeah. I propose we make some use of it. What do you think?"

"I'm on board with that plan," she whispers and kisses me again.

Somehow I keep a hold of her and keep kissing her, while I'm looking past her head to see where the fuck I'm stumbling. It's still savage dark in the room without the candles lit. I bump a hip into the kitchen counter, and when I follow it up with a shoulder bump into the bedroom's door jamb, we start laughing.

I pull my mouth away as her laugh brushes over my lips. "No more snogging till I get us to the bed, yeah?"

She laughs again, and it's making my chest warm to see her so happy.

I grip her tightly with one arm and slap my other against the wall, feeling my way into the bedroom. When my legs bump the bed, I toss her onto the mattress as if into a pool, a massive grin splitting my face.

She bounces against the mattress with a startled laugh and splays out, arms out to her sides like a snow angel, which I can barely make out in the storm's gloom.

"Let me fetch us some candles. Don't be going anywhere, yeah."

"Okay." She whips off her shirt and shimmies out of her shorts. I love how uninhibited she is. She has walls around her still, but in this aspect she's all in, and that's a huge turn-on.

I also love how she fights with me for control of the action. I bang around on the nightstand until I find myself a candle and lighter we put there and get it lit. I also duck into the kitchen and snag my tin. I have one condom left and plan to make the best of it.

A heartbeat later I'm back. Her eyes are on me, and she hooks her thumb into the edges of her white knickers. Before she can wiggle out of those, I grasp her ankles and tug her across the bed toward me. Her eyes widen, and a smile stretches across her face. Her brown hair is fanning out behind her.

I'm owing her some pleasure, but I'm also wanting to taste her.

Badly.

I drop to my knees on the carpeted floor and push her legs apart. I have her where I want her, her pussy at the edge of the bed covered in that white fabric. As I watch, her knickers darken slightly. Fuck me, she's getting wet.

I brush my nose across her inner thigh and inhale her incredible scent of arousal.

"What are you doing?" she squeaks.

"What would you be thinking, macushla?"

"You don't have to do that."

"Oh, but I do."

I nudge my nose against the taut fabric covering the prize and rasp the flat of my tongue up the fabric. She gasps.

I work my tongue up until I find her clit through the knickers and suck it, trying to use the fabric to tease the sensitive skin.

But it's not enough. I'm wanting to taste her.

I'm also wanting to tease her some. Make this last.

So I tongue her against her knickers, until she's jerking and gasping. I hold her muscular thighs apart and rub my bearded chin against the softness of her inner thighs.

She bucks. "Conor!"

"Yes, macushla?"

"More, please."

"Whatever you wish, loveen." She's probably expecting me to do the same action with my tongue, or step it up by removing her knickers, but instead I blow softly against her covered pussy, the wet fabric chilling her a touch. As I'd hoped, she's closing her legs, but I hold them firm. I look up at herself. Across the smooth expanse of her belly, her head's thrashing side to side, framed by the perfect V of her cleavage.

I slip my tongue under the elastic and swipe a taste across her folds. I close my eyes and groan. Fuck, she tastes of pure heaven. Now she's muttering incoherently, and she's pulling on my hair.

Some guys don't care to lick out their girl, but I think they're a bunch of pussies, which I know doesn't make sense, and I've never understood why calling someone a pussy is an insult. Pussies are fucking awesome.

The angle is awkward, and I can't bring my fingers into play to push aside the cloth or, better yet, take it off her, because my hands are keeping my head from being clamped by her strong thighs.

I mean, I love licking her gowl like this, but I don't want to suffocate. Though that'd be one fine way to die.

I risk removing one hand, and sure enough, *wham*, that thigh of hers snugs up against me. I ease aside the crotch of her knickers and tease her clit, watching closely, and, yeah, she loves hard tugs, so I flick her clit, and then I'm sucking it into my mouth. She tenses, arches off the bed, chokes out my name, and I'm lapping her up.

Holy Mother, that was fucking savage.

I let up as the last of her shudders fade. I could never be getting enough of her taste, her sounds.

She tugs on my hair, urging me up.

I spring to my feet and yank off my clothes. God, she looks amazing. Claire is splayed out on the bed, her face looking sated, her limbs loose. And she's staring up at me with hooded eyes.

I rip open the condom and roll it on, giving the lad a good stroke. Fuck, it's going to feel awesome to be inside her again.

I lean down and smooth my hands up her strong, silken thighs, and she places her palms on my forearms, letting her hands slide up my skin as I move closer.

We were feverish earlier, so I'm meaning to take my time. I sculpt my hands around her waist and scoot her back a fraction so I can kneel between her legs. Yeah, I'm fucking massive hard.

I pull off her knickers and cup those plump breasts of hers, flicking her nipples, watching them harden.

She arches into my hands. "Conor." She grips my shoulders and yanks me down.

Since we're both liking to be in control, I shift and sit back on my ankles. The lad is pointing straight up, eager for her.

I lace my fingers with hers and pull. "Up here, macushla."

She scrambles onto her knees, her hands on my shoulders,

and climbs up onto me, ready to ride. This way we're sharing control. The single candle highlights her cheekbones, the curve of a shoulder, the side of her breast.

I hold my cock as she lowers herself. She stops as she nudges the tip, and I rub the head through her folds, finding her wet as ever and giving her clit extra attention. When the head of my lad sweeps back to her opening, she groans and impales herself on me with a shout of, "Oh God, Conor."

"You can 'Oh God' me all the day long," I gasp. I squeeze my eyes shut and clench my jaw because—Jaysus—the sensation of her hot box tight around my dick squeezing me is quare good. Bless me if I know why any boyo likes feeling our cocks sink into something warm, wet, and snug, but the biological imperative means we love it.

We also love friction, but I'm letting her set the pace. I clasp her slender waist. Best part about this position? It puts her fantastic diddies in the ideal spot to…I lean forward. Ah, yeah. I lick the top of one of her breasts and circle the tip of my tongue around her nipple, inhaling the scent from her skin.

"Harder," she says, and somehow I know she means her diddies, not the action going on below.

I'm sucking hard now, giving a soft bite here and there, and she jerks, crying out. "God, yes, just like that."

She lifts her hips off in a shallow move—I'm betting because she doesn't want me to be letting go of her breast. I lavish attention on it and circle my hand inward until my thumb reaches her clit. While she slowly rises and falls, I'm working my thumb hard against her.

Soon she's gasping and squeezing like a vise around my cock, over and over, as she has a drawn out, almost lazy orgasm. I stare in awe at her face, blissed out and pure beautiful.

When her last shudders fade, I'm lifting her off me. She looks down, her forehead wrinkling in adorable confusion. "But you haven't—"

"Hold on, yeah."

I set her down on her knees and scoot around so that perfect arse is facing me. I've never been comfortable flipping my bedmates around as if they're dolls, so *I* do the moving. She glances at me over her shoulder. I can see her debating the idea of me taking the upper hand, but she lowers herself onto her elbows.

Fuck, yeah. I know enough about her to know that ceding control to me is massive.

"You better not be going for the back door, buster."

I laugh. "No worries. Maybe later, yeah." I wink at her. Then I grip her hips and drive hard inside her. I wanted to take it slow, but now I'm a greedy motherfucker.

She gasps, which turns into a gratifying moan, and I ease out. I look down, and the sight of my cock leaving her, coated in her juices, makes heat coil in my lower back. I'll not last.

I adjust her hips and ease myself back inside, looking for that spot.

I must hit it, because she gasps, "Holy shit," and clamps down on me hard. Taking care to be hitting that spot again, I ease out and drive back in over and over in controlled thrusts, urgency flushing my skin hot and tightening my bollocks. The pressure continues to build at the base of my spine, and I grit my teeth, trying to hold back spilling into her.

Claire reaches up and strokes her clit. Her taking charge of her pleasure like that is a huge turn-on, plus it means it'll be a matter of seconds before she'll come as I keep pounding into her.

She cries out with her third, yes, third, orgasm—fuck, yeah!—and she's milking me hard. I drive into her one more time and shout her name as the heat and power of my orgasm streaks down my spine, and I'm emptying, emptying, emptying myself into her.

I can feel the lad jerking inside her, the pleasure drawn out because she's still gripping me. Fucking savage.

I collapse over her back, and we roll to the side, somehow with me still buried deep.

I snug her tight up against me, tucking her bum close

to me. Our breaths rasp in and out as we work to regain our breathing.

Jesus, Mary, and Joseph if that wasn't the fiercest sex ever. And while part of me is feckin' delighted, another part is feeling that familiar panic. This girl, I'm starting to fall for her. I want *everything* with her, but do I have anything to be giving her? In a peculiar way, her directness blunts the panic. She's not someone who'd string a lad along for years if he wasn't making her happy.

And I want to make her happy.

14

Claire

Whoa.

My heartbeats are finally settled, but the sweat's still cooling on our bodies and already I'm getting antsy again. I'm cuddled up with Conor after receiving some spectacular orgasms, and my mind just has to churn with what-ifs and what-does-all-this-mean?

"I'll just be disposing of the condom, yeah." Conor slips from the bed and pads into the bathroom. When he returns, he tucks back up against me.

This isn't just sex. It's more, and I'm feeling a little unsure of myself, which peeves me. I check my walls, though, and they all still feel in place. No urges to change myself just to please him. No twinges of worry that I don't have a model-thin body.

I must have tensed during my mild freak-out—for me—because Conor says, "What has you worrying?"

He strokes my stomach, and I nestle further into his warm body. He smells delicious, like his own blend of unique and unknown scents, which all add up to a concoction called Conor that I just want to eat up. Wow. This is new.

"Nothing," I answer.

"None of that now, yeah." He squeezes my hip.

I turn around and prop my head on my hand. His red hair frolics dark in the candlelight, and a line forms between his brows as he contemplates me.

"Was thinking about how the hospital couldn't reach me at first. And our cell phones will be running out of batteries soon." While not exactly what I was thinking at that exact moment, it does *also* have me worried. "It's scarily easy to forget that there's a hurricane out there."

"Am I keeping you distracted?"

I chuckle. "Yes. And a deadly job you're after doing, yeah," I say in a horrible imitation of his accent.

He gives my butt a light swat, his mouth turned up on one side. "That's a terrible attempt," he says in a pretty good American accent.

I skim a finger around a freckle on his shoulder. "I don't like being out of touch like that."

"You like being in control."

"Why do you say that?"

His face splits into a grin, and he squeezes a butt cheek. "You love being in control when we're riding."

"Riding?"

"Having sex, yeah."

"Noticed that, did you?" But he's not quite right. "Yeah, I like control there. I know what I want, and that ensures I get it."

He envelops me in his strong arms and squeezes tight. "That's a fine thing. And I'll be giving it to you, yeah."

I smile. "And you do. No, I don't think I have to be in control with everything in my life, though. The phone-hurricane thing is a general worry."

"I'm understanding. It's humbling being at a storm's mercy."

"That's it." I nuzzle my cheek back into his chest and hold him tighter, not wanting to examine more closely how safe he makes me feel.

He's quiet for so long I wonder if he's fallen asleep until he says, "Are you thinking it's the storm, though, that's…"

When he doesn't finish the thought, I look at him. "The storm that's what?"

He runs a finger across my cheek. "That's providing the glue." His eyes have gone dark, shuttered.

"You're speaking in riddles. The glue to what?" I whisper, aware in some strange way that this is a delicate moment in getting to know him better. I've always admired his loyalty and dedication to his team, but in the short time we've been holed up in this room, I'm seeing a playful and tender side, and it's doing strange things to my insides. What if…what if I earned that loyalty too?

"The glue to us. It's exciting, yeah, and… Forget it."

My heart does a weird squeeze. *Holy shit.* He's unsure of himself. This big hunky Irishman. "Conor, what's this about?"

"Never you mind." He gives me another playful swat and a grin, but he's not fooling me.

I hitch up higher on his chest so I can hold his face. His embarrassment is coming off him in waves. "I have a confession."

He swallows. "What's that?"

"I've had a crush on you for three years." God, it feels good to admit that. Scary but good. "The storm might have thrown us together in this room, but it's not why I'm in this bed with you."

Conor flips me over until he's caging me in, his weight propped on his elbows. His eyes search mine. "You're being serious?"

"I am."

"Back up a bit. I specifically remember you getting yourself up from a table at the Fado's in Chicago when I joined you and some others and you walking to the other side of the bar. And staying there."

"You remember that? That was last year."

"Yeah. I remember. I thought you were a dead feek when first we met—"

"Dead feek?"

"Hot as fuck, I believe is the American expression. But you

were making it clear you weren't interested. At least I thought you were." He looks at me a moment longer. "Well, you're a hard nut to crack, aren't ya? I had no idea. And believe me, I was looking for signs ever since I first clapped eyes on ya."

An unfamiliar wave of giddiness washes through me. "You were attracted to me even then?"

"Yeah."

I look to the side. "I suck at flirting. I think I assumed you weren't interested in a tough, non-girly-girl and…" I shrug.

"Protecting yourself by thinking you'd seen better on top of a wedding cake?"

I laugh. "Actually, maybe so."

"But you're so direct and open. I figured you'd have no trouble asking for what you want."

"With most things, yes. And when it comes to sex. But if I have it bad for someone, the stakes are higher."

He winks at me. "So you're saying you have it bad for me, yeah?"

"Yes," I whisper.

He shifts to his side and brushes a hand across my bare stomach. "That's brilliant, yeah."

"Conor?"

"Hmm?"

"Why did you ask about the storm being glue?"

He flops onto his back with a sigh. "I shouldn't have asked that."

I snuggle up to him, and he drapes his arm around me, holding me to his chest. "Why not? It's what was on your mind. You can be honest with me."

He's quiet for a moment, and I wait him out. Finally, he says, "I was with a girl back in Ireland. Brianna. Knew her since I was in nappies, and she was my first girlfriend. We were both each other's firsts."

"Sex?"

"Yeah. And we stayed together through college, and I was of a fair mind to marrying her. Was wanting to get myself set up with a steady job first, prove myself. But she broke it off with me shortly after graduating. Knocked me back."

Oh man. "Did she say why?" I have a strange urge to either hunt the woman down and bop her head or kiss her.

"Yeah. Said I didn't have any substance."

I sit up and stare down at him. "I'd like to knock some substance into *her*." God, that's awful. And so this was the embarrassing breakup he blurted while playing poker. "So it made you worry no one would have a reason to want to be with you."

He pulls me back down against him. "Let's not be talking about Brianna anymore, yeah."

"Okay." But it kills me that someone as solid as Conor would ever doubt himself. The mind games we play with ourselves can be harmful. Boy, am I all too aware. I stroke his chest and play with one of his nipples. We're quiet for a time as I absently stroke his skin, content to just be.

"Why'd you leave Ireland?"

He's quiet. His chest rises, and he blows out a breath. "Many reasons. And before you ask, yeah, Brianna was a major one. Wanted to start my life over."

I could certainly understand wanting to wipe your slate clean.

I go to blow out the candles but notice something.

"Oh, wow." I sit back up again and stare at his crotch. I've never seen an uncircumcised penis before. I mean, I'd seen his, but it looked like any other one in the main aspects. But now it's not hard. Well, it's starting to stir, which was what caught my eye at first. "Can I touch it?"

"I won't be saying no to that, but you're acting like you've never seen a man's wire before."

"Wire?" I chuckle. "That's a new one. I've just never seen one uncut before."

I take him in hand and poke the tip, which is almost hidden inside his foreskin, like it's playing peek-a-boo. I pull down, and the head comes fully out to greet me. "Oh cool." I smooth it back up, completely hiding it. And then back down. Which definitely has an effect as he grows hard in my hand.

"We'll have to be getting creative in finishing if you keep with the stroking."

I cock my head.

His handsome features are twisted into a frown. "No more condoms."

"They might sell some in the little shop next to the check-in desk."

He levers up and swipes his jeans off the floor. "Say no more."

15

CLAIRE

I AWAKE WITH a start, bolting upright, groggy and unsure what awakened me. I sit there a moment as my brain catches up with my surroundings and what day it is. I glance around.

Hotel room.

Clothes on the floor.

Heat rushes over me. Oh, yeah. I look to the other side of the bed, and my heart does a weird squeeze. It's empty.

I smooth my hand over it. Still warm. Surely he didn't leave?

"Would you be looking for me, yeah?" a sexy Irish voice says from the doorway.

I yank my hand away and tuck it under my thigh. Now I know I'm blushing. God, how embarrassing.

Conor strolls in carrying a tray, his stride confident and powerful. He has his jeans on, but no shirt. "Could you eat now?"

"Yes, I am actually hungry."

When he lowers the tray over my lap, I catch my breath. He's set a mini table for me—plate, napkin, and silverware. On the plate are two muffins, and he's cut up one of the apples.

Another part of me melts. "Oh wow. This is awesome, thank you!"

He grins. "You're welcome. I'll be but a moment."

He trots out and returns with another tray, settling in beside me on the bed with his own tray over his lap.

"Where did you get the trays?" I didn't see any in our kitchenette. I'm also looking for an excuse to talk—anything to keep the situation flowing as if this is all normal. And by *all*, I mean the sex, waking up with him bringing me breakfast in bed.

"I went down to the foyer for some news and grabbed them from the buffet." He turns his big grin on me and bites into his apple, which he didn't cut.

"Thank you. So what did you find out?" I bite into my banana nut muffin, still light and the right amount of moist. Hmm, I think they put some cinnamon in this one. Delicious.

"Not much of use. Trees down everywhere, and power's still out. There's a fuckton of debris in the car park."

"Still raining?"

"Not a bit of it. Sky's all blue, acting as innocent as a nun."

I'm antsy to get out of the room. "We should go out and help." I need some fresh air but also some space outside this room to sort through my feelings. Last night was amazing—even better than the first time. But also worse because it seemed more intense. And with the breakfast? I need to get my head—and heart—realigned with reality.

After we finish eating, we get dressed and go outside.

Conor wasn't exaggerating. It looks as if we were in a giant snow globe that got shaken up pretty hard. Frankly I'm surprised that there were this many tree limbs so close to the airport. Mixed in are random objects picked up by the force of the wind—trashcans, torn bits of plastic, a shoe, and tons and tons of leaves.

The hotel chain will have their corporate owners pay for a cleaning crew, but it feels good to do something out in the fresh air. We must not be the only ones wanting to help—a few other guests I recognize from the impromptu sing-along last night are outside dragging smaller limbs over to the distant corner of the lot.

We start to help, and while this is mostly giving me the space I need to sort out my feelings—*and* being in a situation that is not sexual certainly helps—it's also relaxing, and the camaraderie with Conor and the others feels great. It also leaves me even more lost, though. As if I'm stuck in limbo, literally and emotionally. We can't go anywhere until that limbo is over, and could the sex just be due to our circumstances? Was this just…limbo sex? *Was* the storm just glue?

A shout jolts me from my ever-spiraling thoughts. "You can't do that!" Some guy from the hotel is running toward us, arms waving.

"We're just wanting to help, yeah." Conor stops and turns to face him, arms loaded with sticks and limbs.

"I know, but corporate will have my head if you get hurt. Can't afford a lawsuit, and I want to keep my job."

Conor drops the load he was hefting and looks at me with his eyebrows raised. "You Americans are so bloody bolloxed."

"I know." I shrug. "Well, we tried."

"Want to go for a walk then?"

"Sure."

Downed trees are everywhere, and people like us are looking around. It's kinda hard not to gawk. On their own, our hands find each other and thread together, the movement so natural, it took me several steps to realize what we're doing. And I know it's stupid to be analyzing *holding hands*, but it feels like a punctuation mark. An exclamation point really. Last night in the lobby, I'd been surprised he'd reached for my hand but chalked it up to him offering sympathy for my mom. This, after the sex last night, the talk after, feels couple-y.

Because, yep, last night was blistering hot. And breakfast in bed was sweet. But as we walk, the destruction reminds me exactly *why* we've been in our own bubble outside of reality. And that reminder is sobering. Everything is temporary.

We don't make it far, though. Conor points ahead. "Sure look it. Downed power line."

"Yikes. Yeah, we better turn back." Dammit. I still need

more time outside—outside where I can think and process and not get pulled prematurely back into limbo-sex land and thinking it can be *more*.

Conor squeezes my hand. "Claire, I want to be asking you something, yeah."

"Sure."

"I'd like to be calling on you when we return if you're keen."

"Call?"

He curses then laughs. "Fucking language. Visit you. Date you, yeah?"

My chest flutters, but I squeeze his hand. "I'd like that. I…like what we've started." Hope blooms, mixing with my panic. Okay. Okay. So it's *not* limbo sex.

As soon as we get back to our room, I call Jane and give her an update on my status.

"Wait," she says. "You're in a room with Conor?"

Honestly. She sounds like a grade-schooler. I pull the phone away from my ear to make sure it's still Jane.

"Yeeessss." I turn around and watch the object of our discussion putzing around in the kitchen. He holds up the packet of trail mix with a raised brow, and I shake my head no.

I fill her in on what happened.

"He's there right now, so you can't talk, right?"

"Yes." Not that I would have said much more, but it's a convenient excuse.

"How about if I ask yes or no questions?"

What the hell? "Jane."

"Come on. Play along. You were all up in my business with Aiden. Payback time."

I groan, which she mistakes for permission, because she asks, "Have you slept with him yet?"

My brief silence as I think how to respond says plenty, because she gasps. "You go, girl. So you guys are a thing?"

I step over to the window and run a finger down the glass pane. "I don't know."

"You don't know?"

I pull my finger off the cool pane and ball my hand into

a fist, resting it against the glass. I lower my voice. "Jane, can you lay off with the questions?"

"Spoil sport. Speaking of. Have you made plans yet to visit your mother?"

Guilt swamps me. *Fuck*. My mother.

I'd successfully shoved that mess into a mental corner, going all ostrich-in-sand. Knowing I can't keep this from Jane, I tell her about my call from the Denver hospital.

"Oh my God. You have to go now, Claire."

My chest tightens with panic. "I know, I know. There's the little matter of being stuck here right now."

"You're still not going to go, are you?"

I zip into the bedroom and shut the door. "Jane, I just..."

"What's going on?" Gone is her frustration. Now her voice holds concern with a trace of curiosity. "Why don't you want to go? You never said—I just assumed it was your usual bullheadedness. But now..."

"Can you trust me that I have reasons? I can't tell you now." I reinvented myself and moved to escape the emotional turmoil of my childhood. And since that childhood represented the old me, I never felt the need to tell even my closest friend. But I'm starting to wonder if keeping my best friend from this part of my life is doing me any good. She knows me well enough now not to see that old, sick me as *me* me. Shame washes through me at what I used to do. And what I had to do.

"Because he's there."

"Yes." I swallow past the lump in my throat. "I'll tell you when I get back, okay?"

"Okay," she whispers. "It must be bad, and I'm sorry I pushed you. We'll go for drinks."

"Sounds like a plan." My words come out fast.

We catch up on other things and hang up.

And I still don't feel any more settled in my mind. Yes, he's saying he wants to continue to date, which makes me feel stupid-giddy, but it also still scares me. Can I still maintain my *self*?

16

Conor

WHILE CLAIRE'S ON her mobile with Jane, mine pings with an alert.

Delta's flying again, thank you, Mother Mary.

I use the last of my laptop's battery and book a flight for early afternoon.

I glance at the closed bedroom door.

And think about why Claire would be mucking about over visiting her mam. The most likely seeming reason to me? Finances. And that'd be the reason most would be reluctant to admit to.

Especially someone as proud and tough as Claire.

Ever since I woke up, I've been doing some thinking. Claire asking about my sister and her farm was bothering me, and as we worked to clear limbs, I realized I'm needing to let my guilt go about the farm. Need to believe in my sister, I do. Believe she knows what she's doing. And that if she ever needs me to lend a hand, she'll know to reach out.

I pour trail mix into a bowl and settle on the couch. God, it hurts to just not help, but I'm needing to do this. For myself and my sister.

But thinking is not the same as doing, now is it? I pull up flights for Denver and use the money I would have sent

Siobhan for Claire's flight, as well as one from there to Sarasota, date of return flexible. Typing in my card number makes guilt flood me anew that I'm using the money earmarked for the farm. Which—fuck—confirms I'm in the right of it. Confirms I wasn't helping Siobhan for the right reasons.

The confirmation screen pops up when the bedroom door opens.

"I've good news," I say, closing my laptop.

She looks at me with her eyebrows up.

"Airport's been cleared for flights."

"Oh. That's...great." She's not looking all that happy.

Thinking it's worry for her mam and how she'll get there, I point to the laptop. "Got you a flight to Denver, yeah." Jaysus. That felt good to say.

"You...wait, what?"

Tension crackles in the air, and I let my hand drop. "To go visit your mam? Didn't you say she's in hospital in Denver?"

She marches into the living room. "You bought me a ticket to Denver?"

"Yeah, sure. What else would I be doing? I figured you'll be wanting to leave as soon as you can, so I booked the first flight."

She puts her hands on her hips. "What the hell? Why would you do that?"

I wince and fall back against the couch. Bollocks. I should've thought this through. If she's too proud to admit she's short of cash, she'll not be wanting to accept something she sees as charity.

I wave a no-big-deal. "Just thought I'd help out a little. A gift, yeah."

"A gift?" Her voice rises on the end.

Shite. I'm making a right hash of things and sounding as if I'm paying her as a thank-you for the sex. *Shut yer gob, Conor.*

She quick-steps to the kitchen in a huff, stops, and marches over to the window and stares out. She rounds on me looking cheesed off enough to skin me alive. Anger blares from her eyes. Her chest is heaving as if she's trying to catch her breath. "You have no right to control my life and what I will and won't do."

Fuck—what? "Control your life?" I leap off the couch. "I'm not—"

"Yes, you are. I told you last night I didn't want to go, and you just ignore that?"

Jaysus, she's lost her head, and this is a right bags now. This is why I'm no bloody good at relationships. Too many minefields, and I'm too dense to scout them out. "Yeah, you said you'd think about it, and I thought…"

"You thought what?"

"That maybe you…" Fuck. I'll just have to say it, because I'm already in deep. "I was thinking you might be hedging on going because you couldn't afford the price of it."

She looks up at the ceiling. "Jesus."

Now I'm pissed off. I was trying to help, and it fucking backfires on me. Part of me can see there's obviously a different reason she's not wanting to go other than money. But that part is swamped by feeling utterly gobsmacked.

Claire

I'M STANDING HERE shaking as memories cascade over me, one after another. Memories of all the times my mom or ex-boyfriend tried to control me, completely overriding my wishes. Why did I think this time would be different? I open myself up, make myself vulnerable, and it's like *boom*— everyone thinks I'm a doormat or that I haven't spoken or that I don't know my own mind.

"You have no room to talk, Conor. You won't even be honest with yourself about why you work so hard to help your sister."

He takes a step back. "Yeah, I'm realizing that. It's why I bought you a ticket."

"That makes no sense."

"I'm using the money I would have sent her, yeah."

"So now you're just transferring your superhero-save-the-day attention to me? I don't need your help. I don't *want* your help."

A pained look crosses his face, and part of me cringes, because I know he's all about helping, but I'm worried about my walls crumbling for him.

"Yeah, sure, but…" He scrapes his hand through his hair and pulls.

"You're just transferring. Don't you see? You help her out of some guilt you feel for leaving the farm, leaving Ireland. What do you feel guilty about with me, huh?"

His hands come down, his brow furrowing and his gaze narrowing. "What the bleeding hell? You've got a maggoting idea there, you have."

"I know you feel guilt about your family farm. It comes off you in waves whenever you talk about it."

"You might have the right of that, but I'm not helping *you* out of some flaming sense of guilt. You're out there."

I clamp my lips shut. Maybe I *have* crossed a line, but I feel hemmed in. Can't he see he's trying to micromanage me like he does his sister?

"Thank you, Conor, but I can manage fine on my own." I can't follow that with *Always have*, which does feel like the next natural line, but that's part of the problem. I haven't. And I got really sick.

I slip into my room and pull up my cell. The next flight available to Sarasota isn't until 8:27 that night. Ugh. A little message icon shows that I have an email. I pull it up, and it's from Delta, with the itinerary shared with me from Conor when he booked the ticket for Denver.

He pokes his head in, his face grim. His duffel bag's over his shoulder. "I'm taking off, yeah. I'll see you in Sarasota,

Claire." His voice is flat, devoid of all his playful charm. He looks as if he can't wait to leave.

"You're leaving?"

"My flight's in two hours."

"Gah. They must have filled that plane. The next one to Sarasota isn't until tonight."

He just looks at me and nods. And without another word, he pulls his head back and shuts the door.

As soon as I hear the outer door shut too, and I know I'm fully alone, a weird ache squeezes my chest. What the hell? Am I already missing him? Already missing the connection we briefly shared?

But that doesn't matter. While it's hard finding the right person that I'm attracted to, I can't be with someone who'll steamroll right over me.

My throat tightens as I slip off the bed and wander into the living room and see the evidence that yes, we hung out here and had a fantastic time, but that time is gone. He's gone. This was just a side road away from our regular lives.

We had fun, but it's over.

It'll be awkward at the league get-togethers, but we can be mature about it. I pace the room, excess energy coursing through me. When I see the bathroom door, I stiffen and step haltingly there as a need to purge hits me.

I pull in a shuddering breath. And release it. Blood pounds in my ears as I stare at that door and what lays beyond it.

I clench my fists. Close my eyes, blocking out the sight. No.

I'm stronger than this. I count down from twenty as I concentrate on pulling in one measured breath after another in time with the count.

God. This only happens lately when I'm at my weakest.

I collapse onto the couch and hear and feel a crinkle. I fish out a bent-up playing card. Jack of Hearts. If that's a sign, I don't know what it's trying to tell me.

Out of curiosity, I open up the itinerary he sent.

The flight to Denver is in three hours.

I stare at that email and bite my lip. I could pack up and head to the airport and catch that flight now or hang out here for eight more hours until my flight home.

The walls feel as if they're confining me. They're also mocking me—a shell that contained the great time we had. The quiet in the room is like a weight, loud in the absence of the sound we made here. Now that we're no longer having fun in this shell, I want to get the fuck out of here.

Yeah. I jump up and look at everything in the room. I'm getting out of here. Out of this limbo. I hustle over to the hotel phone and call the bellhop to bring a box. Thankfully, he has one, and as soon as he arrives with it, I throw in all the unopened food. Wow, yeah, we bought way too much.

With that done, I pack up my own belongings and check out of the hotel, leaving the box of food with the concierge. I call a Lyft and wait for it to take me to the airport. God, I hope I won't run into Conor, though.

If I take the Denver flight, I'll get out of Atlanta earlier. It doesn't mean I actually have to see my mom. I can turn right around and use the return ticket.

Speaks to the state of my brain right now that I don't think this is at all bananas.

17

I'M SITTING NEAR the front of the puddle jumper flight to Sarasota, on the side that only has one seat, which suits me perfectly fine.

The thing with flying in one of these is that you can feel every bump in the air. The flight's not long, but long enough for thoughts to plague me. I boarded the plane still pissed off, berating myself for even thinking things might be developing into something with Claire. This is why I don't date and don't have a go at relationships anymore.

But Claire's words—about my reason for helping my sister—follow me. All during the flight, I poke and prod at why that is, when did it start, and why a flutter of panic rose up when she said she wasn't needing my help.

And I remember that weak moment when I was asking her if the storm was our only feckin' glue. She'd wanted to know why, and I redirected that line of questioning because, Jaysus, it was cutting close to the bone, yeah. It's as if I believe helping others is the only good quality I have to offer. I'm doing it as a way to compensate for some "lack" I see in myself. Evidently, I must have been thinking I was a bit of a dosser for a mother to not even want to stick around.

No. Her leaving was on her, not me.

And I might not have had what Brianna wanted, but it didn't mean there was nothing in me for anyone else to be wanting.

By the time we land and everyone's jumping up to grab their bags, my mood's different. I'm still pissed off at myself but now for a different reason. I stand in the cramped space, sling my laptop bag over my shoulder, and turn on my mobile. If Claire decided to go to Denver, her plane'll just be taking off from Atlanta.

I clamber down the ladder, my steps dully thumping against the metal. My foot hits the tarmac, and I'm breathing in the hot humidity of Florida at high noon. The heat is murder—something my Irish arse still isn't used to.

Palm trees line the landing field of Sarasota airport. I thought taking this job in a beautiful beach city would be compensation for working so hard—a reward—but I'm never having a chance to enjoy it. So how much of a reward is it really, yeah?

I work too feckin' much.

I stomp across the tarmac, hiking my laptop bag higher on my shoulder.

Yeah, my pissed-off flavor has changed to me realizing I've been a complete gobshite. I made a right hames of things with Claire.

I should have trusted she had her reasons for not wanting to see her mother in hospital, and I shouldn't have pushed her.

She's got the right of it. I'm always trying to fix things for people and be ever so helpful.

Heat visibly rises from the black tarmac as I trod to the door they've marked Enter.

Another consequence of sitting on a plane for an hour—montage city, like I was reviewing snippets of a romcom movie, but of my own past couple of days. And that montage? Showed I haven't had this much fun with someone in donkey's years. I've kept myself too busy, and it's all been just a coping mechanism. A way to avoid looking at myself.

Claire helped me find happiness in small moments.

She also seemed to be enjoying my company even when I wasn't trying to help her.

Claire

I'M CRUISING AT thirty thousand feet, white puffy clouds making a landscape as far as I can see.

I'm on the first leg of my flight to Denver.

I have a two-hour layover in Chicago to look forward to. Oh joy.

I shift in my seat and swallow back hot tears. I can't concentrate at all on the book I have in my lap.

I keep replaying that broken look on Conor's face when I said I didn't need his help.

God, I was such a bitch to him.

By sticking to the role I set at the start of my healing journey—estranged from my mother—I hadn't periodically stopped to examine whether it still made sense. I mean, obviously at the start, I believed it was necessary to keep myself healthy. But I just kept that as my default setting and didn't bother to reassess. To question. And I think it's because I was too afraid—afraid to face the emotional memories, afraid I wasn't strong enough not to backslide.

I *am* strong enough to see my mom. I am now.

The earlier, sick me was very weak and very afraid, though.

I lean my forehead against the plane's hull and stare out at the cotton ball sky. The kicker is realizing this now. If I'd realized it sooner, the fight with Conor would have gone very differently. Hell, it might not have even happened, because I would have felt safe telling him of the time I was weak, and so he wouldn't have bought that ticket.

Instead, I'd reacted with my old self—the one who still

thought she was weak. The irony is, it was that fight that showed me I've come farther on my journey to healing from bulimia than I thought. I just hadn't taken that *final* step to realize my own strength and that I can let older coping mechanisms go. Because they're no longer needed.

Conor's gesture to purchase the ticket forced me to express my will rather than suppress it. Proved I'm no longer vulnerable to being a doormat, that I *can* trust that I'll speak out when my desires aren't being considered. I just wish I had recognized my own strength in time to not go all tantrum on Conor, marking my territory, scared to not be in control of every single aspect of my life.

Because if I had? I'd have seen that Conor wasn't trying to control me, only help.

And I know I'm closer to being recovered, because despite wanting to be with him, I took an action I *knew* would drive him away in order to protect myself. I'm no longer someone who rolls over when I have feelings for someone. And I didn't purge earlier.

I do a mental check. And I'm surprised to find that my walls are still there. But instead of having them crumble, Conor's on the inside of those walls.

The shock of that realization has me falling back against my seat.

I can be strong. Be myself. And…

I can have Conor too.

CONOR

JAYSUS. I'M GONE in the head for doing this, but I put myself back on another plane.

Heading to bleeding Denver.

I have no idea if Claire even used that ticket I bought her. For all I know, she's now boarding the plane to Sarasota.

But I'm wagering she's not. And d'ya know, I fair hope I'm right. Here's my thinking—no matter what's going on in that clever head of hers and even with her acting like a hurt animal backed into a corner, she's tough. She'll want to prove herself capable of facing whatever it is that has her scared.

And if I'm right, I want to be in Denver too. To face whatever has her scared with her.

If I'm in the wrong of it, then I might have buggered my chance for the promotion for nothing. I bunked off work, telling them I had to reschedule due to a family emergency.

They weren't happy.

But Claire's more important than chasing money. The bonus, while a fine thing, isn't something I'm needing—I'm making plenty and putting enough aside.

So, yeah, here I am, on a plane to Denver.

Somehow, I manage to take a kip for the rest of the flight, and soon enough I'm pushing through my fellow travelers to exit onto the concourse. I aim straight for the digital display showing incoming flights. I'm going to risk letting my duffel circle in baggage claim so I can stay in this section of the airport and meet Claire at her gate. I could text her, but I'm worried her mobile will have given up by now, and she might not have had a chance to recharge it. I don't want to risk depending on that, plus I'm feeling as if I need to take a fucking risk and be showing her how I'm feeling. If she thinks I'm near, she might avoid me altogether.

I scan the display until I find her layover flight from Chicago.

On time.

I look at my mobile.

Shite.

Not lashes of time. Thirty minutes until it lands.

Of course her gate is on the far concourse. I rush through all the travelers, feeling like a salmon swimming upstream.

I near one of those stores that sells every-fucking-thing a traveler might need and duck inside, hoping in the few minutes I have that something will inspire me. For a gift, you know? I still have no idea what I'm going to do.

My mind's churning in a mad panic. I'm searching the aisles. What's fucking romantic?

But would Claire even *want* something sappy? She doesn't strike me as someone who'd go for the overly sentimental.

Jaysus, I'm screwed.

Maybe if I'd dated more, I'd have a better idea.

Then I see them. I grab the gift and head to the register, even though part of me is thinking, *What the fuck, ya tool?*

Bloody all if I'm understanding how my brain is working just now, but I grab some red heart balloons too, in case this is a rotten idea.

18

CLAIRE

I BUMP ONTO the gangway from the plane and clutch my purse tighter to my side with one hand while the other pulls my carry-on.

Folks crowd the space in front of me with their rollers, their free hands thumbing away on their phones, some still doing the *ding-ding-ding* of repeated incoming alerts that happens when you turn airplane mode off. Through the tunnel weave the strains of some guy singing, which is really weird, but to each his own. I can't make out the lyrics.

I pull out my phone too and open Lyft to see if they're in this city. I booked my hotel room while I was on layover in Chicago, so I just need to take each step as it comes. First, get to hotel. Second, call Conor and apologize. Third, see my mother.

A wisp of worry seeps in at that last step, but I straighten my spine. I'll be fine. I'll be okay. It also reminds me of the distance between us, because I don't know why she's in Denver.

It's only as I get closer to the gate that the singer's lyrics penetrate. My hairs stand on end. The guy's voice is clearly singing the lines from "Total Eclipse of the Heart." Memories of Conor and me playing that weird form of strip poker swamp me.

God, my throat. It's getting all swollen and shit.

I must be allergic to something in this godforsaken tunnel.

Ha. Who am I kidding?

Regret hits me, deep and hard. Conor and I parted so horribly. Hearing those lyrics—now—man, that has to be a sign.

Whoever the singer is, he's trying admirably to hit those gutsy notes, but it's not quite working. He doesn't seem to care, though, as he keeps going gamely on.

When I clear the door of the gate, I stop.

Holy shit.

I swear, my heart does this weird swoopy thing and then falls straight through my stomach. It's probably a big, throbbing, bloody mess on the floor, because the guy singing is *Conor*, and he's looking at his phone as he belts out the lyrics, a plastic bag in his other hand.

He's also holding a bouquet of heart balloons. Several women are standing around watching, wistfulness in their gazes. Some of them are chiming in with the "bright eyes" chorus at the appropriate moments in the song..

I choke on a half-sob, half-laugh, which he hears. He looks up, smiling hugely, but even through the glisten in my own eyes, I can see the worry and vulnerability in his light green ones. My heart squeezes right then and there. He's obviously unsure of his welcome, but he doesn't let that hold him back.

Conor

MOTHER MARY, I'M trying to project confidence as I belt out this tune, but inside my guts are tied in fucking knots.

There's more riding on this presentation than I've ever had before. Add to that the fact that I have not a ball's notion how it'll go over and I had bloody all time for prep.

But sure, I'm feeling as if I have to do this, not only for her but for myself.

Shite. She's just standing there. Unmoving. Her eyes wide. I glance back down to get the next line from the song, and my voice is faltering, but I'm not quitting.

A *clunk* sounds in front of me, and I glance up. Claire's let go of her carry-on and is lurching forward, but she takes a hopper over her bag. She stumbles toward me, trying to recover her balance, and I catch her.

As her skin touches mine, everything inside me notches back into place. She looks up at me, her eyes glassy. She opens her mouth, but before she can be saying anything, I tell her, "Wait."

She arches a brow.

Of course there's a ring of folks around us watching, but I'm not letting that stop me. I do, however, lower my voice. "I'm sorry I didn't take your feelings into account. I should have trusted you at least enough to know you'd be having a good reason for not coming here. I shouldn't have been making assumptions, yeah."

I hand her the plastic bag and the balloons. "Got you these."

She looks in the plastic bag. Closes it. Then looks up at me, confused. "You got me panties? White panties?"

My heart's beating like mad, while my brain is going, *You gowl, muppeting plonker*, over and over. But I soldier on. I take a deep breath. "Yeah. I was wanting you to know I like you the way you are."

She tilts her head, and the eyebrow goes up again. "And white panties say that? Is that one of the designated couple gifts for anniversaries? I don't keep track of those things."

I laugh. "Yeah, sure. Never hide from myself. That's what they're saying." Since she still looks confused, I continue. "That first night, I saw you tuck your knickers out of the way when you showed me around the hotel room."

She blushes a beautiful shade of pink, and her eyes get big and tender. And it says volumes that I even notice that shite. And then, thank fuck and all the saints, she's standing on her toes and planting one on me.

Cheers break out all around, and since we're giving them a grand show, I give in to what I really want to do—I cradle her face and return that kiss with one of my own, pouring into it all the hope and relief I'm feeling in this fine moment.

19

AN HOUR LATER, the Lyft driver drops us off at my hotel. We didn't say much in the car, just logistics. We held hands, though. I think we both needed the time to absorb what this all means.

I know I needed that time. I mean, this is huge, him just showing up like this, and my heart's fluttering in excitement and panic, and I want to make sure the excited part of me prevails.

Maybe that's also why I need the time too.

Plus, I still have things I need to tell him.

We register and make our way up to the room. Inside, it's a standard hotel room, no business suite like we shared for several days in Atlanta.

Conor throws his duffel on the floor. "You hungry, yeah?"

My stomach growls. "I think that's a yes."

"You grand with ordering room service? I'm famished, but I don't want to be going out, yeah. I'm just wanting to be here, with yourself."

Okay, now my stomach does that fluttery thing, but this time because *holy shit*. "That would be nice." I sit down on the bed, run my hand along the bedspread, the cool surface calming, and look at him. "I need to tell you something.

115

About why I freaked out like that."

He takes a moment to look at me. "Sure."

"But let's order food first."

So we pull out the menu and place our orders. We settle on the bed, sitting cross-legged across from each other. I take a deep breath. "I was a bulimic."

Conor straightens his spine but remains quiet. I like that he's not acting all shocked and immediately asking questions. He gives me his full attention, knowing I have more to say.

Before, the urge to share had been strong, but I'd stomped on it. Too afraid. Now I let that urge free, because Conor's been understanding even when he didn't know—setting the table, being considerate inside and outside of the bedroom.

I look to the side. "I was on the fast track for Olympic trials for the US sailing team back when I was in junior high."

"Well enough. And something happened, I take it?"

I smooth my hand across the comforter and make a starfish pattern. "It wasn't something I actually wanted, but I don't think I fully understood that then. It was something my mom wanted, and so, by extension, I did too. To please her. And she saw my chance at the Olympic team as the financial golden ticket. She raised me by herself."

"Where was your da?"

I glance at him, already steeling myself for the standard pity, but I see only curiosity, and maybe a touch of sympathy. "I don't know. And since I never had one, I don't really miss one?" I shake my head. "That's not quite right. I do in an abstract way. I wonder what it would have been like having one. But it was always just my mom and me. She has a… strong personality."

He chuckles. "That's not surprising me."

"Yeah, well, I wasn't me then."

He cocks his head to the side.

Yeah, okay, that sounds odd. "What I mean is—how you see me today is not how I was then. In fact, it's *because* of what I went through, and had to do to heal, that I am the way I am." I edge closer on the bed, stalling. "And it's…it's also why I freaked out on you. I was a bit of a doormat as a preteen." I look at him and wince.

His forehead wrinkles, his eyes confused. "I can't see you being much of a doormat."

I wave a hand to the side. "I was. I let my mom overwhelm me, and her desires came to be mine. Therapy helped me realize all this and that I'd also been trying to conform to a certain body type I thought I should have with a swimsuit on. I was always in a swimsuit. Well, anyway, to deal with the stress, I'd eat. It was another girl at school who showed me the trick"—I air quote—"of throwing up after eating a lot. At first, I only did it if I ate too much. But then I wanted to slim down and…you can guess the rest."

I was always chasing after my mom's body shape. She was tall and lean like a super model. And I didn't look anything like her. Since getting healthy, I can now see our resemblance, of course, but as a kid, I felt like the ugly duckling next to the swan. Brown-haired and chunky next to her ethereal blonde.

Conor takes my hands. "You're saying you made yourself unhealthy."

I swallow. "I did. So much so that I failed the trials." His strong, warm hands ground me.

"Sure, and how did you break free of the cycle then?"

I take a deep, shuddering breath. "That was a wakeup call. I got help from a counselor at my high school. But the real headway came when I broke ties with my mom and moved to Sarasota, to start my life over basically."

We're interrupted by a knock on the door, and we take a break while we set out our food, designating the middle of the bed as our table.

After a few minutes, Conor wipes his mouth and sets his napkin down. "You're a fine thing, you know. Utterly incredible."

"Because I broke off with my mom?"

"Because you found in yourself the strength to do what you were needing to get yourself healthy. I would never have guessed you had food issues in your past. You enjoy your meals as far as I can see."

I look at our plates and smile. "I do. That was part of my recovery, learning to have a different relationship to food than just seeing the calories. It wasn't easy, but I learned to take joy in the food itself, and to listen to my body and trust it. It's why I don't eat on the run either."

"You set the table and turn off the telly."

I squeeze his hands, grateful I don't need to explain. I also feel a rush of warmth because, even before he knew any of this, he didn't make fun of me for setting the table and instead was sweet enough to incorporate it already into our meals together. My body's also asking for something else—a special dessert—so I leave room in my stomach.

"Exactly."

"I've always seen you, in a good way, mind, as having bollocks of feckin' steel." He grins and takes another bite of his burger.

I snort. "Why do guys think balls are tough anyway. One good smack, and you're down for the count."

"I've given that some thought."

"Why am I not surprised?"

"Bollocks are an important topic, mind. I'm thinking it started precisely because they're so vulnerable—takes a lot of guts to put your pair out in full view where they might get lamped. Hence 'balls of steel,' as you Americans say. But over time, the lads started assuming having a pair made them tough, which it doesn't."

"You might be onto something." I look into his eyes. "And I'm sorry for freaking out. I think what it did was show me how far I've come, though. Part of me hadn't quite shifted to understanding I was recovered. I had to put up such a shell around me so that no one could ever control me like that again, that I kind of got messed up on its purpose. I think I started feeling as if I had to be tough all the time—that I couldn't ever give up control, or I'd get overridden again."

"So when I…"

"So when you bought tickets for me to visit my mom after I said I didn't want to…"

"I wasn't trying to control you, yeah. To be honest, I was thinking maybe you were too proud to be asking for money."

"I know that now. But at the time, I just saw it as someone else ignoring my wishes and steamrolling over me."

He opens his mouth.

"Wait. I need to finish." I take a big breath. "I think in my mind, I thought in order for me to stay healthy, I could never cede control to anyone. But you helped me see that I was quite capable of standing up for myself. And I think I'm ready to admit I'm healed enough that I don't have to be so vigilant about being tough all the time."

"Ah, g'on. Just helping you—it makes me happy, yeah. We can stay the night and fly home in the morning."

I shake my head. "I'm going to see my mom. You helped me see, too, that I was acting out of fear. Deep down, I think I was afraid that I'd backslide if I saw her again. But I need to do this. I need to see her, because if I can see her and remain healthy, I need to." And then I finish on a whisper. "She's my mom."

20

CONOR

I'M FLOORED BY everything Claire's just been telling me. I knew she was tough. The best kind of tough. But I hadn't realized how hard it's been for herself to get to where she is.

I'm also feeling rather lightheaded, because we're here in the hotel, talking, and we've not fallen out.

Claire peeks up at me. "You know how I said that I've learned to just eat what my body's wanting, without questioning it or judging it?"

I nod.

"Well, I have a craving," she says, her eyes going a little sultry. My dick pops against my zipper.

"Yeah?" I clear my throat because that came out a little strangled. "Yeah?"

She purses her lips, and her eyes get a wicked-arse gleam. "Yes. For dessert."

I curse my thoughts for heading in such a direction. Right after she told me all about her bulimia and her mother. My dick has no business getting its hopes up like this, that she'll be riding me soon.

She reaches for the hotel phone and hits a button, looking at me as she waits for the line to pick up. She says to me, "You like chocolate?"

"Yeah, you?" I'm doing my best to earn a fucking award for being supportive.

"Good." She raises the mouthpiece after a second. "Yes, one chocolate cake please. Thank you."

She hasn't broken eye contact the whole time, even now as she lowers the phone.

"Awesome," she says. "Because I have plans for that cake."

Could be because we just had a heavy blathering, but we go on talking about the other times we've been in Denver. One of which was when we came here as a team to play Denver's Gaelic football and hurling teams.

There's a knock on the door. I take our used tray and tip the guy and bring in the cake. It's one of those fancy slices, with shaved chocolate on top of the chocolate icing.

"On the bed?"

She nods.

I climb on the bed, passing her a plate and napkin roll and taking mine. I set the cake in the center.

She looks up at me. "Can you lie down?"

"Lie down?"

She nods. There's a wicked gleam in her eye, which I'm liking.

She pulls the plate holding the slice of cake out of the way and scoots our plates farther apart. She pats the center of the bed. "Right here."

Of course I comply. I have an idea of what she intends, but I don't want to make assumptions. Heart thudding, I stretch out full length and flick my gaze up at her. She lifts the cake and studies my body laid out before her like I'm her personal banquet. She tugs on the hem of my T-shirt, and I yank it off.

"What are you doing, Claire?"

"Me? Just setting the table."

"Setting the—?" I stop because she tips the cake right onto my stomach, the cool frosting hitting my skin and making my abs clench. I grin. "Wicked girl."

The scent of chocolate fills my nose.

She stretches out beside me, but with her head level with the cake. She props her chin on her hand, and her feet kick into the air, lazily swinging backward and forward. She pokes her finger into the icing and scoops up a dollop, catching my gaze. Slowly she brings her finger to her mouth and sucks the tip free of chocolate.

I groan as all remaining blood rushes to the lad, which is growing hard as a fucking rock, fighting against the denim of my jeans for freedom.

She dips her finger back into the icing and this time drags her finger up my chest, painting a trail of chocolate up to my nipple. The icing runs out before she makes it there, so in she dips again and places a dollop on each nipple. I suck in a breath at the cool smooth texture, already anticipating her lick to remove it. Bloody hell.

My hips buck, and she giggles.

She breaks off a chunk of the cake and reaches up until her fingers touch my lips. I part them on a groan, and she tips the bite into my mouth. I close my lips around her finger and suck it clean, while the burst of rich, decadent chocolate cascades across my tongue. A hint of cherry follows after.

Already, she's teaching me to revel in the various tastes of food. "Mmmm. Fuck."

"You like?"

"Not a bit of it. More like loving it." Never thought I'd see food as sexy.

She breaks off another bite and, holding my gaze, puts it in her mouth. Then she leans up and circles her tongue around a nipple, lapping up the icing. I shudder. *Jaysus.* She does the same with the other. Then she rasps her tongue across and sucks it clean, and now I'm fisting my hands at my sides, because fuck, that feels savage good.

She tips another bite into my mouth, and before I can lick it inside, she's crashing her mouth onto mine, and we're both devouring that morsel and each other. My lad is now so hard I fear for its life.

She pulls away and licks her lips.

"Claire, you're ending me."

She grins. "You like it."

"Fuck, yeah. How could I not?"

She laughs again. Then she inches down my body, cleaning up the icing she painted across me earlier with her wicked tongue.

She props her head on her hand again, and with her free hand, she unbuttons my jeans and lowers my zipper. She looks up at me and raises a brow. I nod like a feckin' kid being asked if he wants candy. I think I know what she's asking, and I'm more than ready for her.

To eliminate any doubt, I lift my hips. She sits up on her knees and yanks my jeans down, taking my butt-huggers with them, while I'm toeing off my trainers. When she gets the jeans to my calves, I help her by kicking them free and then yank off my socks.

She tosses my jeans to the side and changes her position, this time laying her body perpendicular to mine so her head is right by… I glance down. And then thump my head against the pillow and close my eyes briefly. Right by *my* lad's head.

I open my eyes again, though, because there's no fucking way I'm missing another second of this.

She scoops some of the rich cake onto her fingers and smears some on the crown of my cock. It jerks, and I groan. She takes another scoop and slides it into her mouth, her tongue licking up stray crumbs across her lips. Then she places another in my mouth. By now the cake is barely discernible as a slice, but it speaks to how moist the cake is because it's not just a pile of dry, broken crumbs all over my stomach and the bed.

She takes the last ridge of icing left and paints it down my cock. Then she leans down, and I hold my breath. She catches my gaze, her eyes twinkling, and then at the last second, she switches her trajectory and eats a bite of cake straight off of my stomach. My whole body tenses as her tongue laps up a second bite there.

"Want the last bite?" she asks.

All I can do is nod.

She scoops it up and places it on my mouth, with her lips just a second behind. She closes her lips around mine, and we share the taste of that chocolate cake together, and I've never tasted anything better. *Angels in heaven, have mercy on me.*

The delicious morsel is soon devoured, and my hands are in her hair, holding her head in place as we taste, nip, stroke, and it's driving me wild.

She breaks away and licks her lips.

Then, Jaysus, she scoots down, licks my stomach clean, and I tense. Sure enough, she strokes that devil of a tongue down my lad, and my hips lift off the bed. I let out a groan.

Then she grips my base and pumps it, holding it up like it's her own personal, chocolate-covered ice cream cone.

She takes her time cleaning every last bit of icing, and it's all I can do not to paint the ceiling with my cum, because, yeah, it feels like I'd reach that high. My hands are in tight fists, and every single muscle is tensed.

I glance down. "Clean enough," I growl. And pull her up by her shoulders.

"You're still sticky." She looks as if she's pouting, and my dick does a little kick of appreciation.

"They make these brilliant things called showers, yeah. My vote is we hop in. Together." I drag my eyes up and down her body. "Because I'm thinking you're dirty yourself."

Her eyes flare with heat. "I think I'm dirty too. And sticky. Down there especially."

I groan and jump out of the bed, practically running into the adjoining bathroom. It's a monstrous tiled step-in shower with a glass wall and a large showerhead. Oh, and it must be Christmas, because there's a separate handheld showerhead.

Footsteps follow me inside, and as I open the door and lean in, her warmth kisses my back, and then her sumptuous body presses against me. Correction. Her *naked* skin presses against me.

I twist the handle and put my hand under the spray. "How are you liking it, macushla?"

"Hot and hard."

My dick jumps, and I laugh. "I was meaning the water."

Her voice is all innocence. "I was talking about the water, big guy."

She reaches her hand in, and we get the temp just right. I step inside and stand under the spray. She's not inside yet, and I peek an eye open.

Claire's grabbing the little bottles off the sink counter. Oh yeah. "Good thinking."

She steps inside, her eyes flashing with heat, and closes the glass door behind her. I place my hands on her hips and step us around in a half-circle until she's under the spray. She leans her head back, letting the water soak her hair, and the rivulets of water are running down all of her delicious curves. The water's doing exactly what I want to do—exploring every inch, caressing her skin.

I smooth my hands up her waist and turn her so her back's to me and her face is out of the water. I grab the bottle of body wash and squirt some into my hand. "Where are you dirty, macushla?"

She hums and pushes her bum against me. She takes my hand with the body wash and runs it down her smooth belly and into her short curls. I wrap my other arm around her chest and pull her tight against me. Fuck, she feels savage good—all warm, wet skin. I flick her clit and brush my fingers against her folds. "Yeah. I'm thinking this area needs extra attention."

"If you say so," she breathes.

With the body wash and her own arousal, she's slick as a seal, and I flick and rub until I find the right combo of speed and pressure that has her gasping. She splays her hands against the tiles and pushes that round bum of hers into me as I finger fuck her. It's all I can do not to slip my cock into her, but we haven't had a conversation yet on no condom, and I'll be buggered if I'm stopping to ask about tests and birth control.

With my free hand, I grab the handheld showerhead and turn it on. As she's writhing against me and my hand, I direct the pulsing spray on her pussy, and she cries out.

Her orgasm overtakes her, and she's milking my fingers. Her knees buckle. I drop the showerhead, letting it bang against the tile, and wrap my arm around her waist, holding her up while I keep fingering her, drawing out her orgasm. Hiking her up against me, I nibble her neck and slowly ease up with my fingers.

"Jesus," she gasps out.

I give her one last swipe. "I think you're clean now."

She spins around, and I steady her. She's giving myself a savage grin. "Your turn now."

21

MY LEGS ARE like jelly. Damn that man can give good finger.

I squirt the body wash into my palm, rub my hands together, then skim them up and down his chest. His muscles bunch and flex in the wake of my fingers, and it's like having a living work of art in front of me—all hard lines of sculpted muscle narrowing down to his jutting cock.

Eating that cake off him was the best table setting *evah*.

Now the remnants of the chocolate I didn't get with my tongue are sluicing off his chest and cock. I squirt another dollop of body wash into my hand and grip his girth. I press up on my toes and nuzzle his neck and ear lobe as I work his length between our stomachs.

He tenses all over and widens his stance, bracing a palm on the wall behind me.

I find the rhythm that makes his hips and moans go wild, and when his hand grips mine to try and pull it away, I know he's close.

I pull my head down until my forehead rests against his upper chest and I can look down at my hand, which I refuse to allow him to pull away.

God, I can't wait to have him inside me again. Oh, wait. I still and look up.

"You're finally understanding now, yeah?"

This time I let him pull my hand away. I nod. "Then hurry."

"Hurry?"

"Yeah. With the cleaning. Can't use a condom in here." Thank God I don't have to explain, and we rinse off in record time.

He jumps out of the shower and skids across the tile, righting himself against the counter.

"Be careful!" I grip the side of the shower door, water dripping off me onto the floor.

He snags a towel, throws it at me. I snatch it, and we both rub ourselves down as if our lives depend on it. Then we race into the room. I jump onto the bed, and he dives for his duffel. The crinkle of a condom wrapper being opened fills the room. It's as if I've turned into Pavlov's dog, because that sound now has me clenching.

I also remember there are crumbs on the comforter. I've no sooner yanked it off and pulled the cool sheets back than I feel his hands at my waist and his cock pressed against my ass.

I moan. "Fuck the sheets," I say.

"Yeah. Fuck the fucking sheets."

He lifts my leg up, resting my knee on the edge of the bed. Oh yes. I fall forward until my hands hit the bed. My skin, hot from the shower, feels as if it has extra nerve endings or something because every brush of his skin along mine is driving me wild.

And I ache. "Hurry."

"Always wanting to move your arse faster than is wise." He laughs. "Is this"—his hard cock shoves into me, and I gasp—"fast enough for ya?" He pulls out, the friction heating me everywhere.

"Yes. Don't stop."

He plunges back inside, over and over, and I've never experienced the term "fuck like bunnies," but this has got to be it. We're reduced to grunts and slapping thighs, as we both chase our release.

I can no longer hold myself up by my hands and drop

to my elbows. The position has me not only open, but he's able to drive deep into me. I reach up and rub my clit, hard, as he thrusts inside me, and that's all it takes. Pleasure roars down my spine, and I'm spasming around him so hard it hurts. But a good kind of pain.

"*In ainm Dé.*" He grabs my waist and shoves into me hard, one more time, and I can feel him jerking inside me.

We both collapse onto the bed, breathing hard, and he pulls me up against him.

He squeezes me once. "Don't be moving a muscle."

"I don't think I can." Everything in me is languid heat.

He moves off the bed and pads into the bathroom. The toilet flushing is immediate as he disposes of the condom.

Soon, he's back by my side, and we snuggle up against each other as we're catching our breaths.

It feels great to be here, with him. His stomach growls, and I snort. "We just ate."

"An hour ago at least. And I didn't have lunch. And we did have a bit of a fair workout, yeah."

Soon we're sitting on the bed while he eats another burger and fries, chatting about the upcoming championship games for the men's team. Unfortunately for my women's team, we don't have enough numbers to compete, so we're out of the running.

Then he says, "Sorry, Claire."

"For giving me a mind-blowing orgasm? Anytime, buddy." I pat his knee.

He's quiet. I quickly glance up. Oh, he's serious.

"No, for pushing about you visiting your mam."

"I understand. We're good."

"No. I think I need to tell you why. My...my mother..." He pulls in a sharp breath and slowly lets it out. I push aside his plate, and we snuggle on the bed, me holding him tight because I can feel the emotion coming off him and how hard this is.

He swallows. "She left us when I was around being seven. I don't care to think about it much, because why should I dwell, yeah? But I think hearing about your mam and how you weren't going to be seeing her, it triggered something. If your mam—"

He breaks off and looks at the ceiling.

I think I know what he's getting at but can't say. "If I have a mom who wishes for me to be in her life, I shouldn't throw that away."

He looks at me and brushes a hand down my head. "But it's your life and your decision." He pulls a strand away and looks at it. "I'm here for you whatever you're thinking is best."

My heart does this weird squishy thing. "Thank you."

22

LATER THAT NIGHT, we're walking down the sterile hallway of the hospital. I called and received permission to arrive after visiting hours. Conor has a tight grip on my hand. I asked him to come along, not because I need him as support but because it feels natural.

I push open the door of her room. The early evening sky makes up the far wall of her room, and a single bed in the center is hooked up to a bunch of beeping monitors. I pull in a breath and let my gaze travel up from her feet to her head. And there she is.

My mom. Whom I haven't seen in five years.

She's awake, and she's staring at me with round eyes. She bites her lip. I can feel the tension in the room, and some of it's new—tension of a reunion, of not having seen each other in too long of a time. But most of it's familiar tension.

All my memories of feeling inadequate, of not being enough, rush back.

Even hooked up to an IV and one of those nasal oxygen things, with wires snaking to monitors, she's still beautiful, graceful. I guaran-damn-tee you if I was in her place, I'd have crusty drool, flat hair, and under-eye bags or something.

My mom claps her hands across her stomach. "What

happened to your blonde hair?"

I haven't seen her in five years, and that's the first thing she asks? I shunt aside the familiar irritation. "I stopped dyeing it, Mom."

She's silent, and the usual judgment seeps into the space between us, keeping us apart. She's not happy that I'm no longer dyeing my hair, but I'm okay with that. I no longer see it as a failure I need to rectify.

She reaches out a hand.

I squeeze Conor's hand, then let it go and close the distance to her bed. I clasp her hand, bend over, and give her a kiss on her cheek and an awkward hug, considering she's laid up on the bed all hooked up to stuff. More memories swamp me as I inhale her scent—still the same soap and perfume, though blunted by the general odor of hospital.

I squeeze her arm. "How are you feeling?"

"Been better."

She looks over my shoulder, and I turn around and wave Conor inside. "Mom, this is Conor."

"Nice to meet you, Conor. Sorry it's like this." As always, she's all proper, and she manages to look regal and poised despite being laid up in a hospital bed connected to all these devices.

"I'm sorry too, ma'am. And the pleasure's all mine."

I turn back to my mom. "What does the doctor say?"

"I'll be fine. Mostly shook up."

"What exactly happened? They just told me you were in a car accident."

"Some jerk T-boned me running a red light. Air bag deployed, so it's mostly bruises and scrapes. I did hit my head on the side of the car, so they're keeping me for observation, but I'm supposed to be released tomorrow."

"Why did they keep you so long then?"

She looks to the side.

"Mom?"

"Turns out I had what they're calling a 'mild cardiac incident.' Some kind of blocked artery. There's a stent in there now, and it's all repaired. Doctor said that it was fortunate I had the accident because they might not have caught it otherwise."

All I can feel is relief. At all of it. "That's good."

Conor clears his throat. "Would anyone care for some tea or coffee? I'm going to make a run for myself."

My mom and I shake our heads, and Conor looks at me with an eyebrow raised—a silent question.

"I'll be fine," I whisper, and he nods.

As soon as the door closes, I turn back to my mom. "Why are you in Denver?" I ask softly, feeling guilty that I don't know the answer.

"I moved here two years ago for a job." Her eyes range over my face, and then she starts crying. Given that it's my mom, they're genteel tears, not great, ugly sobs, but they're real.

"I'm sorry, Claire. I didn't know."

I cock my head to the side. She knew I was sick.

"What I put you through when you were growing up. I just…I just wanted what I thought was best for you, but… it wasn't until after you cut yourself from my life that I went to see a therapist."

"You did?" That floors me, because my mom used to call them quacks.

"Yes. She helped me see what I did by pushing you like that. I was just…scared. Money was tight, and I…"

"You thought the Olympics would be a great way to secure our finances." And "tight" is a relative term. We were solidly middle class.

"Yes." She swallows. "Can you forgive me?"

I pull in a deep breath. "Yes. And I'm sorry. For leaving and cutting you out of my life. I had to, to…" Now it's my turn not to be able to finish.

Mom squeezes my hand. "To protect yourself. I understand. I didn't have the right…coping tools to help you get better."

There's still healing to be done in regards to my mom, but…

But this is progress.

And maybe, just maybe, I can also forgive myself for having to do this. For having been too weak to do anything other than cut her completely from my life.

At a noise at the door, I turn and see Conor's head peek in, and warmth blooms in my chest. I could have faced coming here on my own. But I'm also really glad he's here too. Conor gets me, and I'm still my strong self.

Which is an amazing gift.

Conor

I'D WAITED UNTIL I heard the murmurs inside the room quiet down. Until I heard some tentative laughter. Then I'd pushed open the door. I wanted to give Claire space with her mam.

And I'm ready to leave and give her more if she's wanting that.

But Claire turned to me. Now she smiles, but it's a weak thing, barely lifting her mouth, and somehow I know the wet of tears I'm seeing in her eyes isn't about me, but more for this situation with her mam, and I'm welcome to come in.

A nurse comes in behind me, and I step aside.

The older woman asks Claire's mam her name and birth date, checks her vitals, and records them in some handheld digital thing. Then she gives her some meds.

She turns a stern eye on Claire. "She needs her rest."

"What time will she be discharged tomorrow?"

"We won't know until the doctor clears her tomorrow."

Claire steps to her mam. "We'll see you in the morning, okay?" She kisses her cheek.

Her mam pats her hand and murmurs something I'm not hearing. I hold my hand out, and Claire places her palm into mine. I clasp it, enjoying the connection with herself again, and lead us out of the room.

When the door closes behind us, I slip my arm over her shoulder. "Let's go, stinky feet."

Claire gasps then laughs. "I don't have stinky feet."

"Sure I know, but I still love picturing you at the airport, legs all bent and looking like you were catching a whiff of your own feet."

"I'll never live that down, will I?"

We stroll down the hallway, and I pull her up snug against me. She feels grand by my side.

"Nope." I lean down and kiss that spot right behind her ear. On cue, her neck turns pink. As we find our way into the cool Denver evening, I whisper in her ear what I'd like to be doing when we get back to the hotel.

And while her reaction is everything I could wish for, what I really love is this feeling right now. Here. In this moment. Because I find myself more comfortable, and more myself, next to her than ever I have before with anyone else. That's giving me hope that together we'll sort out whatever issues we might face.

This connection with her—I'm not sure I believed I deserved it on its own. Not without feeling like I had to earn it.

THE END

Thank you for reading Claire and Conor's story. and I hope you enjoyed their journey to love as much as I did writing it! If you missed the first book in the series, check out Earning It! To be alerted to my releases, be sure to join my newsletter on my website, www.angelaquarles.com.

ACKNOWLEDGMENTS

I'D LIKE TO thank the following folks who read early versions and helped me make this a better story! Jami Gold and Shaila Patel. You guys helped me to not only craft a better story, but also helped in the cheerleading department too. Thank you!

I'd also like to thank several of my readers who also read early versions and gave me helpful feedback: Megan and Courtney, thank you!

My editors Gwen Hayes, Erynn Newman, and Julie Glover had my back again, which I appreciate so much.

I'd also like to thank several people I consulted with regarding bulimia and eating disorders: Laura R. for reading the whole and giving feedback, and August McLaughlin for answering extensive questions before I even started writing the first draft and for answering the odd question during the writing and editing phases. She has an excellent blog at augustmclaughlin.com and has a book releasing the summer of 2018: *Girl Boner: The Good Girl's Guide to Sexual Empowerment* (Amberjack Publishing), which includes her eating disorder story and a lot about body image.

To Shannon Donnelly and Zara Keane for helping me with Conor's speech patterns and expressions, I appreciate it big time! County Galway has one of the highest percentages of Gaelic speakers and his cadence would reflect that, as well as the occasional Gaelic word thrown in.

I also want to thank the members of my facebook fan group for their help and support!

I'd also like to thank my facebook and twitter friends who are always willing to answer questions I pose, whether it's about writing, or character ideas, or an opinion sought.

And finally to my family, who have always believed in me and make it possible for me to pursue writing.

ABOUT THE
AUTHOR

Photo by Keyhole Photography

ANGELA QUARLES IS a RWA RITA® Winner and *USA Today* bestselling author of contemporary, time travel, and romance. Her steampunk, *Steam Me Up, Rawley*, was named Best Self-Published Romance of 2015 by *Library Journal* and *Must Love Chainmail* won the 2016 RITA® Award in the paranormal category, the first indie to win in that category. Angela loves history, folklore, and family history. She decided to take this love of history and her active imagination and write stories of romance and adventure for others to enjoy. When not writing, she's either working at the local indie bookstore or enjoying the usual stuff like gardening, reading, hanging out, eating, drinking, chasing squirrels out of the walls, and creating the occasional knitted scarf.

She has a B.A. in Anthropology and International Studies with a minor in German from Emory University, and a Masters in Heritage Preservation from Georgia State University. She was an exchange student to Finland in high school and studied abroad in Vienna one summer in college.

Find Angela Quarles Online:
www.angelaquarles.com
@angelaquarles
Facebook.com/authorangelaquarles
Mailing list: www.angelaquarles.com/join-my-mail-
ing-list